MOUNTAIN SHADOWS

MARIE CAMPBELL

iUniverse LLC
Bloomington

MOUNTAIN SHADOWS

iUniverse books may be ordered through booksellers or by contacting:

iUniverse LLC
1663 Liberty Drive
Bloomington, IN 47403
www.iuniverse.com
1-800-Authors (1-800-288-4677)

ISBN: 978-1-4917-2802-4 (sc)
ISBN: 978-1-4917-2803-1 (e)

Library of Congress Control Number: 2014904481

Printed in the United States of America.

iUniverse rev. date: 03/05/2014

Chapter 1

The whole mountain seemed to be frozen. White on white. The snow had fallen week after week. Then it had frozen solid turning the mountain into a white wilderness.

High in the pale sky a buzzard appeared searching for food in the white waste. There was nothing. No sign of any movement. It circled around then flew off round the shoulder of the mountain.

Colin Grant looked around. In the distance was the village he had walked from, Dunree. He had only arrived that morning. He couldn't wait to get onto the mountains. He booked a room in the village inn and as soon as he changed into warm clothes and sturdy boots he had set off. He breathed in. What he had been told about the Highland air was true. It did feel so pure. He felt his whole body coming alive with the real joy of it.

He had left Edinburgh that morning. His friends at the university had tried to persuade him to go to Paris with them. They were all celebrating passing their finals. He had qualified MA (Medicine) with Honours but he preferred to visit the Highlands. His father had spoken often of his ancestors going back many generations.

He had started to do a family tree but going back to his great grandparents was as far as he could get. After that, try as he might, it seemed as though the Grants never existed. But as far back as he could track it would seem that they may have been round about this area in Dunree which was as deep in the Highlands as one could get.

He was so deep in thought that it was some time before he realized that his walking had got easier. It seemed that he had been walking up a frozen burn. So much easier than the steep hillside. He followed it over a low ridge. He stopped to rest and look around. He was expecting to see nothing, just the same whiteness all around. But then to his surprise a few hundred yards away there was a house.

Or maybe that was too much calling it that. It was more like a shack. One small window each side of the door and a corrugated iron roof. A ladder was leaning on it as though as though someone had been doing repairs on it. To the side was some sort of enclosure, maybe used to keep animals. He felt a strange feeling looking down at it. He felt that he wanted to get away from that area. Then a few flakes of snow started to fall. Why am I feeling so stupid he thought to himself? I could go and maybe get shelter till this snow shower passes.

He gave a timid knock at the door and shouted "Hello." When there was no reply he reached up to a little space above the door and found a key. He placed it in the lock and was about to turn it to go inside when he hesitated. How did I know that there was a key hidden there and once again he got the feeling to get away quickly from the area?

He turned and made his way back the way he had come.

The snow started to fall in earnest. By the time he arrived back at the inn it was turning into a blizzard.

"Well glad to see you back safely." Jim Dounie the inn keeper met him at the door. "It's always a worry when someone goes alone into the mountains. You look pretty frozen. There is plenty hot water if you want a bath. Dinner will be in half an hour. We only have two other guests staying. This is quite a quiet time of year." Colin turned to go upstairs. He turned back. "Mr. Dounie could you tell me something about an old derelict house a good way up the mountain?"

Jim Dounie turned back. "Come into the lounge after your dinner. I will have time then to have a talk with you."

When he entered the dining room only a couple about his own age were having a meal. They introduced themselves. The man, about six foot, a boyish look about him with fair curly hair and bright blue eyes. "I am Kevin Shepton and the midget beside me is my sister Sally." there was a strong resemblance between them. The same fair hair and blue eyes. Sally laughed. "Maybe I am a midget but I can sort out big brother." In actual fact she was probably about five foot six. They had strong American accents. Colin introduced himself. "I have booked in here for three days to do a bit of hill walking. I am a New Zealander. I have just finished my final year at Edinburgh." Sally smiled at him showing beautiful perfect white teeth. It made Colin's heart flutter. "What did you do? she asked. "Oh Medicine." "You must be a very young Doctor?" "Not really. I am twenty six." Her brother laughed. "There you are Colin. My sister always wanting to find out information." "Now brother dear. Only about people that interest me." Colin felt himself blushing. "How about joining us for a drink in the bar after dinner? Kevin suggested. "Yes why not. But I must have an early night. I'm going hill walking again tomorrow early."

After dinner Colin went to the lounge to talk to James Dounie. He found him sitting by the fire sipping a beer. "Can I get you a drink?" "Well no actually I am going to join the American couple in the bar but I am dying to find out what you know about the house that I came across today."

"Well Colin, I really know very little. I only bought this inn about a year ago. This is one of the strangest villages I have ever been in. My wife died three years ago in a car accident. Ever since I have been wandering around. Not been able to settle anywhere. I wandered into this village and saw the For Sale sign. The price was right. Much cheaper than I expected and on the spur of the moment I bought it.

I meant it when I said it was a strange village. You would think that as it's the only pub that it would be a friendly place to be sociable to visitors. But it's the opposite. I bet when you go into the bar the young couple will be sitting alone and all the locals at another table. No talking, even amongst themselves. No laughter. It's like being in a church. An old man comes in about nine o'clock. I found out his name. He is called the Keeper. He doesn't have a drink. He whispers something to the men and they all get up, finish their drinks and go."

One day I met the Keeper when I went looking around the village just after I arrived. He had a cottage just on the village boundary. I told him that a couple staying at the inn were very interested in an old cottage high up on the hill. The same one that you are interested in. They wanted to know its history. Well I must admit I was totally taken aback at his reaction. He waved his walking stick at me. Tell them to keep away or they will regret it. For a moment I thought he would hit me with his stick. An old tramp like man with his long hair which looked as if it hadn't seen a wash for years. But he was well over six feet. Big broad shoulders. I beat a hasty retreat. We now just ignore each other. But believe me there is something strange going on."

Colin made his way to the bar. Jim Dounie was right. The couple was sitting apart and four or five men were sitting. They had a drink in front of them but there was no conversation. He bought himself a beer and joined Kevin and Sally. They were quite subdued. The atmosphere in the pub was getting to them. Kevin tried to get a conversation going. "So you came all the way from New Zealand to go to Edinburgh University. A long distance Colin." "Well it really was only for the final year."

"I did it for two reasons. First of all I had always wanted to study in Edinburgh and secondly I think it made my father so happy. He had never managed to visit Scotland and so many stories had been handed down throughout the generations and he was so disappointed that he couldn't trace further back than his great grandparents. And trying to piece some bits of the stories I think they must be fairly near this area."

"Well I think we will retire. This air does make me sleepy." Sally turned to her brother. "Are you coming?" Kevin finished his drink. "Yes I'll be with you in a minute." He shook hands with Colin. "We will maybe see you in the morning but we are leaving early. We are going skiing to Aviemore. Enjoy your walk tomorrow Colin and take care."

Colin was left sitting alone. Finishing his drink he looked up when the door opened. A strange looking man entered and from Jim's description this was the Keeper. There was something gorilla like in the way he walked. And the length of his arms. It was difficult to guess his age. He just stood at the table beside the men. He must have said something. Colin couldn't hear but the men all stood up and followed him out of the bar. Maybe there was a simple explanation. They could be poachers. But why go into the bar. Colin gave up and made his way up to bed.

Next morning he entered the dining room early. The young couple had already gone. Jim was serving breakfast. "No point in taking on anyone when we are so quiet. And of course the American couple only had juice and cereal. "Well," Colin said. "I would like a full breakfast if that's possible. It will fortify me all day on the mountain." "No bother," Jim said. "I will also make you some sandwiches and fill a flask." Colin thanked him. In some way he felt sorry for him. He seemed to be quite lonely. He was stuck here in a village that wasn't very friendly, still mourning the loss of his wife. Maybe when the summer season came he would be too busy to be lonely. "Remember now," he shouted after Colin. "Don't take any risks."

Colin started off. He had decided to explore the opposite side. Once again he felt a wonderful form of release, the snow sparkling in the sun. And as he left the village behind, the peacefulness, as if he was the only person in the whole world. If anything this route he had chosen was much steeper than the previous day. After a couple of hours he felt himself getting a bit breathless. I really am out of condition. All the hours I sat indoors studying hasn't helped. He decided to sit and have some coffee from the flask. The heat of the sun reflecting off the snow made him feel quite drowsy.

He thought he felt the smell of wood smoke. Can't be. Who would be lighting a fire high up on a snow covered mountain. But the smell persisted. Then he saw a thin trail of smoke wafting towards him in a soft breeze. It seemed to be coming from just round the corner from where he was sitting. He scrambled to his feet and in his excitement he very nearly fell over a ravine because he couldn't believe his eyes. Standing in quite a large wood was a huge building almost like a gothic castle.

The smoke he saw was coming from some of the large chimneys. He felt he was dreaming. Yesterday he had come across a ramshackle house and today a castle. He was so busy looking at it that he wasn't watching where he was putting his feet. He tripped and tried to stop himself falling but down he came. He felt something hitting his leg and when he tried to get up he realised that he must have twisted his ankle. He had hit a rock partly covered in the snow.

The shock hit him and he just sat there. He started to feel the cold. I have got to move. Then panic set in. How am I going to get home? How will anyone find him? He had his mobile phone. He pulled his bag towards him. He could give directions saying he was in sight of a castle. There was nothing on his phone. Then he realised that it was nearly two days since it was charged. What a fool he was.

"Well you have landed yourself in a bit of a pickle," a voice above him said. He turned round. The man standing near him had the look of a Highland estate worker. He was tall, nearly six feet. A full beard nearly covered his piercing dark eyes. He was wearing a heavy tweed jacket and plus fours. He held out a walking stick to help pull him to his feet. "If you use the stick and lean on me we might manage to get you to Fast castle."

"How did you find me?" Colin asked.

"Oh I didn't find you. The Master Sir Nigel Grant spotted you through his binoculars. Told me to come and get you before you froze to death."

"I am sorry to be such a nuisance." "You can say that. Do you realize that you are on private property? You weren't spying by any chance?" "Of course not. Why on earth would I be spying?" "Well it's not the first time I have had to chase away some of the nosey ones from the village."

They had arrived at huge iron gates. Two large fierce dogs, he thought maybe Alsatians. They growled and showed their teeth. They were guarding the gate. His rescuer shouted at them and they quietened but when they went in the still prowled round them daring them to make a wrong move.

Chapter 2

Colin felt a bit disappointed that instead of going to the castle he took him into a little gate house. It was pretty basic. Two armchairs each side of the fire. A table and chairs. A dresser. Lots of crockery. It was obvious that he lived there alone and when he opened a door into his bedroom looking for his first aid box. Colin could see that it was just as sparse. Only a bed and a wardrobe and a chair that seemed to be full of clothes just dumped there.

The two dogs had followed them in and lay stretched out by the fire. But as soon as he moved their heads shot up. The man came out of his room. He had found the first aid box. He filled a basin with hot water from a kettle beside the fire. When he thought it was the right temperature he told him to put his injured foot into it.

"I'm sure it's not broken," Colin told him. "I think it's just strained. I'll be all right when the swelling goes down." "Is that right," said the man. "And how would you be knowing?" He was being sarcastic. "Because I am a doctor," Colin said. The man just grunted and proceeded to bandage his foot.

"Now if you just sit there I'll go and get the snow mobile and get you back to the village."

What a strange place and what a strange man. Imagine having a snow mobile. But I suppose it does make sense, living so high up the mountain.

In a few minutes he was back and helped him into the mobile. There was a bit of a rush. It wasn't meant for two large men. Colin held on for dear life as they whizzed down the mountain. In no time they arrived. A few hundred yards from the village near the boundary fence.

"You will have to make your way from here," he said. And before Colin could ask his name or thank him, he had turned and in no time he was gone.

He managed to limp toward the inn. Nobody came to offer to help him but he felt that they all watched from behind their curtains. Jim Dounie came out to help him.

"Come in. You look as if you could do with a drink." He pulled the chair near the fire and placed a large brandy in his hand. He sipped it slowly and felt his body relaxing. Jim was desperate to find out what had happened. "How did you get your foot bandaged? What happened to you on the mountain?" So as Colin told his story Jim's mouth opened up bigger and bigger. "A castle you say. I have lived here for nearly a year. I have never heard of a castle. "Well no wonder there is a fence round the estate. No one dare enter and there are dogs. I just happened to stumble into it."

"Well you have certainly brought a bit of excitement into my life," he said.

For a couple of days he rested his foot. By the third day he was so bored. The sun was shining. He just had to get out. Jim let him borrow his slippers and with the aid of a walking stick he was able to hobble outside the door of the inn. He found a seat and was quite happy to sit down. The sun shining on the snow was really warm. There didn't seem to be anyone around. Such a pretty village. When the foot bets better in another few days I must go exploring it. He estimated that there could be about three or four hundred living there.

Just as he had decided to go back inside he saw a figure walking in his direction. As he got closer he saw that it was the Keeper looking much the same as he was in the pub. When he was alongside Colin called. "Good morning." But he just ignored him, carrying on past looking straight ahead. It made him thing again about the strange incident in the pub when the four men all got up and followed the keeper without a word being spoken.

A few people had arrived. They looked like him with the gear they were wearing, ready to walk in the mountains.

His eye was taken by a girl talking to the new arrivals. She really was something to look at. Tall, chestnut coloured hair tied back in a pony tail. Her face, slightly tanned, seemed to emphasise the brilliant blue of her eyes.

She gave a tinkling laugh at something one of the parties said. Her whole body seemed to be full of the joy of life.

Colin went to look for Jim to ask about them. He was busy cleaning the bar. "I do hope the girl comes in today to work a few hours. The rooms need to get ready for that party. They have booked in for three days." "So who are they?" Colin asked. "Oh they are from a rambling club from Glasgow and it's a bit of a nuisance because they all want single rooms. I only have two and you are in one. They will have to pay extra for using the double rooms.

I really shouldn't be complaining. Things have been so quiet. I am grateful for the business. So, Colin thought to himself. Single rooms. That means that the lovely lady isn't married and the three men with her can't be involved.

He shook himself. What am I thinking about? It's as well my friends are not here. They would have a right laugh at me and they would be right. Maybe it's something to do with the sun and snow that's making me think like a young schoolboy.

Well no matter. I will probably see them at dinner tonight. Then another thought. Did he have a clean shirt to wear?

Chapter 3

The party was already in the dining room. One of the men shouted over. "If you are on your own would you like to join us?" They made room for him. "You have had an accident," one of the men said. "Was it on the mountain?"

Colin explained what had happened but something held him back from telling them about the mansion house or castle as he thought about it in his mind.

The woman turned to him and smiled and once again Colin thought how beautiful she was. "You must be awfully bored just hanging about all day? she asked.

"Well I won't be able to go on to the mountain but I'm going to go exploring the village tomorrow." She stretched out her hand. "I am Carol Houston. My friends are Peter, George and Richard. We all belong to Glasgow and to the same club." Colin told them that this was his first visit to the Highlands and that he had been studying in Edinburgh but his home was New Zealand. "Ah," Carol smiled. "I just couldn't place your accent."

After dinner they all trooped into the bar. The four men were at their usual table, not uttering a word. And as usual the Keeper came in, whispered to them and as usual they all got up and left.

"A pretty weird crowd. Do they never speak?" Carol asked. "No never. Jim the owner told me not since he bought the inn over a year ago."

After breakfast the men set off. Carol decided that she would rather stay behind and if Colin didn't mind they could go exploring the village together.

Colin was delighted to have her company. His ankle and foot were much better and with the help of a walking stick he was able to walk quite comfortably.

"It really is a pretty village," Carol said as they walked down what appeared to be the only street. Little cottages, all freshly painted, lined it. "Let's go into the church," Carol said. "I just love old churches." And this one was certainly very old.

"I think it is Episcopalian. Look there is a golden eagle in a star." The walls were granite. Just left the way they were when it was built, with no adornments. The only colour was from a large stained glass window above the altar. An organ near the back of the church seemed to be in good tune. A plaque near the organ proclaimed the building of the church to 1612.

"Gosh it is old. No wonder it feels so damp." And with that old smell they were quite happy to get back out into the sunshine. Further along was a school but it seemed to be deserted. No sound of children. In fact there was no sound of children anywhere in the village. "Could be holiday time or maybe the Pied Piper took them all away," Carol said

Chapter 4

Near the village square there was a little café. "Would you like a coffee?" Colin asked. "It would warm us up." The bell pinged on the door as they went in. There were only three tables covered in some kind of oil cloth. A counter which held a glass case with a few tired looking cakes. A girl of about sixteen came through from the back. She could have been quite pretty with her doll like face if it hadn't been covered in thick make up.

"Yes what do you want? And before you ask we only have tea or coffee. No cooked food. That lazy bugger out the back never went to get supplies.

"I heard that." A middle aged man came through pulling up his braces on his trousers, his feet encased in a pair of old slippers. He turned to the girl. "Don't you talk to your father like that my girl. Especially in front of customers." Colin and Carol looked at each other. Each knew what was in each other's mind. "Let's get out of here." But they were too late. The girl plonked two coffees and a jug of milk on their table. "Sorry no tea bags. It has to be coffee. That will be three pounds. The father tried to make conversation. "Are you staying long? I suppose you are at the inn?" They nodded. "Nobody stays long in this village," he said. "Only the mountain draws them. There is nothing else." He shuffled off back into the back.

Colin and Carol made a hasty retreat. "Well that's one café we won't be going to again." And when they were out of sight of it they collapsed laughing.

On their way back to the inn they passed the village pond. It was frozen solid. "Poor old ducks. It will be a long time before that pond thaws out."

"I wonder if it was used to duck witches in the old days," Carol laughed.

Colin couldn't believe how lucky he was to spend a day with such a beauty that was also so full of fun.

"I haven't asked you Colin what your work is." "Well at the moment absolutely nothing. I have just graduated as a doctor and in the next few weeks I'm going back home to New Zealand to visit my parents. Then who knows."

"What about you? I think maybe I'd guess at you being a model."

She gave a hearty laugh not like the tinkling one he heard earlier.

She stopped walking and saluted him. "I am Carol Brown, Inspector, from Strathclyde police. And the men with me are all policemen. We are all out to relax and have a good time. It's important to get away from work. So please I would prefer you didn't mention it. People can be so strange if they knew we were all police."

"I have really enjoyed the day with you Colin. If you are fit how about going into the mountains tomorrow?"

"Sure. Nothing would keep me back."

It was a jolly crowd that met in the bar that night.

The four men still sat at their usual table. And the same routine. The Keeper arrived and they all got up and left.

Richard, one of Carol's friends said, "What a rude bunch. How about following them to see where they go." "Not on your life," one of the others said. "Remember we are on holiday."

13

Jim joined them when he finished his chores.

"What is it with this village? No laughter. Everyone going about with grim faces."

"Look I know very little as I told Colin. I have just been here a short time."

"Where are all the children?" Carol asked. "When Colin and I passed the school there didn't seem to be any children in it."

"That's because they all go to school in the next village. They only seem to come home at bedtime. Maybe there are more facilities there for them.

This village is owned by Sir Nigel Grant." "Maybe a relative of yours," someone said.

Colin laughed but something was going on in his head. Was it something his father had said?

Anyway," Jim went on. "He is not a very popular person. He never comes near the village. He has some men servants who come to the village for supplies. Big hunking men they are. Sir Nigel and the Grant family for hundreds of years have lived in Fast castle. No one ever goes near it. There is high fencing and from what I hear fierce dogs guard it.

Lots of rumours abound about the Castle. The usual ones about it being haunted. It is believed that Sir Nigel has a son who visits occasionally. Sometimes there is the sound of a helicopter, presumably belonging to the son, landing at the castle.

It is all very strange that with all the servants at the Castle, absolutely no gossip comes from it. Once when a walker ventured quite close to it he swore that he heard the screams of a woman. But it's possible that he may have heard some old person in the village discussing old folks love stories."

"Oh well this is all very interesting Jim but I'm for bed. Tomorrow is our last day. I noticed that a thaw has set in and with the heat of the sun of the last few days it will be a quick thaw. We will be off early tomorrow Colin" As they all shook hands Carol stayed back. In her forthright manner that Colin had got used to in the four days he had known each other, she said. "I like you Colin. I would like to see you again. Will you keep in touch when or if you come back from New Zealand?

Chapter 5

Colin pulled her close. He felt her trembling when he kissed her. Her lips were soft as the petal in a rose. "Nothing on this earth will stop me seeing you again," he whispered. "My very special Cop."

He felt lost when they had gone. Nor could he believe how quickly the deep feeling he felt for Carol in such a short time.

He still had a couple of days left of his booking in the Inn. He made the most of it, going into the mountains every day.

One afternoon he went into the next village. It was bigger than Dunree and it boasted a very up to date library. He was determined to learn as much as possible about the area. He really didn't know where to start. Then he remembered his father saying that he only managed to go back a few centuries, then absolutely nothing of the Grant family in that Highland area. His father had been right. There was nothing. No births, deaths or marriages. He traced some of the other people who had lived centuries before. All their details were entered. An old man who seemed to spend most of his days in the library approached him.

"Can I help you? Are you looking for something in particular?" "Well, just trying to trace my ancestors." "Well son why don't you go to the church. They have records that go back hundreds of years. What is your name by the way?" "Colin Grant," he said. The old man stepped back. "Go away. Clear off." He shuffled out the door.

Colin was completely taken aback by the old man. After getting over the shock of his rudeness he felt so angry. He ran out after him to demand an explanation. He hadn't gone far and when Colin put his hand on his shoulder he whirled round. "I told you already go away." And Colin got the impression that the old man's face showed fear as well as anger. Has this whole village gone mad? He decided to go back to the church.

The old man had said that village records went back hundreds of years. It seemed such a long time since he was in there with Carol. Only yesterday they had enjoyed exploring the village. But neither of them enjoyed the church. It seemed to be gloomy and smelling of dampness, as though it was hardly used. He remembered that they had been quite happy to get back out into the sunshine.

He got the same feeling again when he went in. He heard a cough behind him. "Can I help you?" Colin jumped. "Sorry," the man said. "I didn't mean to startle you." "That's alright. I'm afraid my thoughts were far away. I did not hear you come in. Are you the vicar?" he asked the man.

The man smiled. Well at least there is someone pleasant in the village he thought. "No I am afraid the church doesn't have a vicar. I am only looking after it. I open it in the morning and lock up at night. We are waiting to get a new vicar since the old Rev Mr. Morrison passed away."

"Do you think you could show me the church records? I want to try to trace my ancestors."

"Of course," the man said. Taking him into the vestry he produced a key to a cupboard. There seemed to be hundreds of books in it. "Was there some particular year you were looking for?" He tried to explain to him. "Well I'm sure there will be something here. I will leave you to browse. I'm Andrew MacFarlane. My house is just two doors away. When you finish you could bring the key to me.

Colin started to go through the church records. He was there for so long he started to get cramp. There was absolutely nothing about the Grant family. He pushed the ledgers back into the cupboard. A sheet of paper, yellowed with age, was stuck at the back but the writing was still legible. He read

Their name be cursed

I cannot allow their name

To contaminate the good book

All Ten Commandments were broken

The Devil was let loose by that

Cursed name

One day the bearer of that same name

Will wash away the sins of the fore bearers

And only then can their name be entered

And peace will return.

Colin sat shocked. Could it be the Grant name?

Surely not. Of all the names the Grant name stood out with honour.

He quickly replaced the paper where it had lain at the back of the cupboard. He took the keys back to Mr. MacFarlane and made his way back to the inn.

He desperately wanted a drink. He had just sat down when his phone rang. It was Carol.

"Colin what are you doing tomorrow? I have got the whole day off. I would like to show you around Glasgow. I could meet you at Buchanan Street bus station if you don't want to drive in the snow." Colin replied immediately. "Great. Looking forward to it."

Carol was waiting when he arrived. Gosh she is so beautiful. How could I be so lucky? She gave him a hug and before he knew what was happening they were in a passionate embrace, her arms round his neck pulling his head down to meet her hungry lips.

When they broke apart they were breathing heavily, looking at each other, saying nothing. There was no need to talk. They walked hand in hand from the bus station. After a while Carol looked at him and smiled. "Now I must show you my Glasgow."

The whole day seemed to pass in a blur. Colin was amazed at how much Carol knew about the history of the city she loved. She took him to Glasgow University. "I know it will be of interest to you. A lot of famous people studied there. For instance Joseph Lister, a surgeon and founder of today's antiseptics. James Watt, inventor of the steam engine." And so it went on. Colin could have listened to her all day. She was all serious one minute then her laugh would break out at some incident.

At night they dined by the side of the River Clyde, eating fish and chips. As the night drew in Colin realized that he hadn't booked in anywhere to stay.

"Don't worry. I sorted it out when you said you were coming." Colin looked at her. She said. "No Colin. I go back to my own digs. In fact I will head off as soon as I see you into yours. I am on early shift so I won't see you before you go back to Dunree. How long are you going to be there? I have got a few days leave starting in a couple of days. I would love to go back to Dunree to be with you." Colin gave a shout of joy. "You are a wonderful girl. I look forward to seeing you again."

On the way back to the village he got a few odd looks from some of the passengers on the bus because he kept smiling to himself.

The next morning he went off again to the mountain. He had such a lot to think about. He knew that he was getting close to Carol but there were so many things to think about. Everything was happening too quickly. He would have to find a practice that would take him on. He would have to start repaying his parents for all the help financially they had given him. He would have to go home soon to New Zealand. Would the feelings between him and Carol survive the separation? His mind kept going round in circles. He hardly noticed how quickly the snow was disappearing from the lower slopes.

Here and there little burns that had been completely frozen under the snow were emerging, the water trickling as it pushed through the frozen ground finding their well known trails down the mountain. Colin stood, taking it all in. He felt such sadness knowing that he would have to leave all this beauty behind. On his way back to the inn he met the Keeper. He didn't bother to talk to him. Before I leave the village I am going to find out what all the ill feeling is about he promised himself. It was as if there were shadows lurking in the shadows and even more so on the mountain.

The next morning he rose early. Carol was arriving from Glasgow on the early bus. He was too excited to eat any breakfast. He walked to the bus stop to meet her. When she walked off the bus he caught his breath. She really was so lovely. Her chestnut coloured hair seemed to glow in the sunshine. Gosh how lucky I am he thought.

They didn't speak. They just put their arms round each other. There was no need for words. They both knew that they had to make the most of the short time together.

Later in the day they decided to explore the other part of the village. It was quite lonely with only a few cottages scattered here and there. Then they came on a strange building. It had all the appearance of a prison. It looked as though it had been recently built.

A high fence surrounded it. It was all on the one level. Windows all the way round but they had bars on them. As they got closer to a high gate and looked through they saw some men. They were busy working in the garden.

Colin gasped. He recognised some of the men. They were the men who sat in the pub every night, not talking. All getting up when the Keeper appeared. They still weren't talking, just getting on with their work. Then they noticed a sign. PSYCHIATRIC ESTABLISHMENT.

Colin and Carol looked at each other in amazement. Then Colin pulled at her arm.

"Look Carol. Look at who has just come round the corner." It was the Keeper. He was wearing some kind of uniform. Navy trousers and a sort of gherkin jacket and a shirt with a red tie. The hair still looked scruffy but what a difference from the one they saw every night in the pub.

"Come on let's get out of here." Colin pulled her away. "Well I'm definitely going to find out what's going on. Why build such a place? And those men. Going to the pub every night. An even Jim, who has been here over a year, knows nothing about them." Then she looked at Colin and smiled. "Well I am a police officer and when I get back to Glasgow I'm going to find out about this village. It's still within our policing range."

They made their way back to the pub. "What a strange place that was," Carol said. "I wonder if they will be in the pub tonight as usual. And the strangest part of all was the Keeper being there.

Colin put his arm round her. "Let's forget about them all. Let's just enjoy the short time we have together." The sun shone on patches of snow at the roadside making it twinkle like hundreds of diamonds.

Carol stopped walking and bent down beside the hedgerow. "Oh Colin just look. Aren't they the most beautiful thing on this earth?" What she had spotted was a cluster of snowdrops. "No wonder they get called the heralds of spring. I think they will bring us luck. Maybe a way will be found one day to let us be together. Colin's spirit lifted. Carol was right. He felt that come what may they would find a way to be together.

That night Colin waited for Carol at the bottom of the stairs to go in for dinner. They were the only ones in the dining room and Jim did the serving. He asked them what they had done with their day and when they told him about the psychiatric building he was amazed. "I never knew such a place existed," he said. "But then I don't do much walking about. Do you think it's for insane people?" "We don't know," Colin said. "It wasn't called a hospital just a psychiatric establishment." He

21

was more amazed when they told him that they saw his customers the four men working in the garden.

Jim's mouth opened in astonishment. And when they told him that the Keeper was also there it was too much for him. He pulled out a chair and sat down. After a minute he said. "They didn't see you did they?" Colin reassured him. "But I wonder if they will appear in the bar tonight.

After dinner Carol and Colin couldn't wait to get into the bar to see if they would arrive. They were already seated at their usual table when they went in. They already had a beer beside them. Jim was serving behind the bar. Colin went up to get the drinks. He whispered to him. "Listen Jim who comes to the bar to get the drinks for the men and who pays for them?"

"Oh," Jim said. "I should have told you. The Keeper has an agreement with me. I have to keep a table for them and he pays me. I also have to bring the drinks to them. It's very awkward. When I put their drinks down in front of them it's just as if I'm not there. In fact when thing start to get busy it's going to be awkward keeping that table for them."

"Have you never spoken to the Keeper?" "You are kidding. The Keeper talks to no one unless it's to snarl at them. Even the villagers keep well clear of him and that's why I am so amazed when you say he was in the garden at that psychiatric place. I just don't understand this village. It gets more and more weird."

It seemed no time that Colin was at the bus stop saying goodbye to Carol. There was such sadness in him as he walked back alone to the inn. Carol promised to find out what was going on in Dunree. Meantime he would keep his ears and eyes open.

He walked again on the mountain and soon the peace and stillness soothed him. The snow had gone apart from high up near the castle. It would probably be there well into the spring.

The stillness was suddenly broken by the sound of a helicopter. It was directly overhead, hardly moving and instantly he knew that he was the object of the surveillance. It moved off heading in the direction of the castle.

He remembered Jim saying that the son owned a helicopter. So many questions were going round in his head. It was so frustrating. There seemed to be mystery after mystery. The one uppermost in his mind was the visit to the church. Why there was no record of any of the Grants and what did it mean when he had found the sheet of paper in the vestry. It was written in such a way that the name of Grant was somehow cursed. Would the bearer of the Grant name do something to rectify the harm they had done.

The more he puzzled over those words the more worried he became. What was the terrible thing that the Grants had done to last for centuries? But then some of the highland clans still held a grudge. Like for instance the MacDonalds of Glencoe and the Campbells. Their feelings went back nearly three hundred years.

The Grants must have done something really bad in and around Dunree. And then of course Sir Nigel Grant and his forbearers owned the village and the surrounding area. Colin shook himself. Best to forget all about it. Soon he would be on his way to New Zealand. As he approached the inn there seemed to be a lot of activity round the door. A group of people were coming out of a bus. Tourists, he thought to himself. Jim would be happy with the business. There were about fifteen of them crowded in the bar. Colin smiled. They were such a happy crowd. One of the men spoke to Colin thinking he was a local.

"This is one of the bonniest places that we have stopped at in the town." Colin couldn't make out his accent. "We have the sea in Aberdeen but you have the mountains."

Then one of the men pulled a mouth organ from his pocket and started to play an old Scottish air and the whole party started to sing. Colin felt a lump in his throat. This was Scotland. The real Scotland.

The door opened and in came the Keeper with the four men. They just sat down at their usual table. Once they were seated the Keeper left. Jim brought the usual beers to their table. It was then Colin noticed that Jim had put a reserved notice on the table. He must have done it before the crowd came in. The talkative man approached the table

"You are local. Can I get you a pint?" The four just stared at him and continued to sip their beer. He came back to Colin. "A queer set up that. How come they are all deaf and dumb? And that queer guy that brought them in. Was he their minder?

Colin was flabbergasted. How had no one noticed that they were deaf and dumb? Not even Jim. But then the Keeper did all the talking. It took the man from Aberdeen to suss it out in minutes.

After about an hour the bus driver came in to shepherd them all back onto the bus. Colin was sorry to see them go. They really did lift his spirit. They were all so happy. But cheering himself up he thought about Carol. He would phone her in the morning. She would be as amazed as him to learn about the four men. He would tease her. Some police inspector she was, not noticing they were deaf and dumb. Mind you they weren't really bothered about them. They were only interested in each other.

He waited to get the phone call from her. She had told him not to ring her. She couldn't have her phone engaged in case there was an emergency.

Jim was in good form. Maybe that bus load could be the first of many. "To tell you the truth Colin I was getting near the edge with money and I had decided to call it a day. As you can see I get no support from the villagers." "Do you think that maybe these strange men sitting there night after night might be putting them off?" "Maybe you are right but what can I do? I can't tell the Keeper to stop taking them in. In fact I would be a bit afraid saying anything to him. God knows how he would react."

Colin's phone rang. It was Carol. He moved out to the door to take it. He just loved to get to talk to her. After a while she got on to the subject of the village. "Not an awful lot to report unfortunately but talking to one of the senior officers I got the impression that they already had an interest in the village. I have a few hours off in the afternoon and I will visit the old crimes department. I believe that they can go back a few hundred years, even as far back as the Jack the Ripper case. I wish I could be there with you Colin. I know that we have only known each other for a short time but I know my feelings for you are true and deep. I will ring you tomorrow my darling."

"I feel exactly the same about you Carol. Do take care and keep yourself safe for me."

He retired to the lounge to write an overdue letter to his parents. He was feeling happy and relaxed by the fire. It had been so good talking to Carol knowing that she felt the way he did.

He became aware that someone had entered the room. It could have been the cold draught from the open door. He turned round and saw a man sidling in looking furtive as he scanned every corner of the room. Eventually he sat at a corner table as far away as possible from Colin. He pressed a bell on the wall and after a couple of minutes Jim came in. He spoke to the man. "How are you tonight? Is the café busy?"

Then Colin recognised him. Of course. This was the father of the bad tempered girl. Jim asked him what he was drinking. He ordered two glasses of whisky and a half bottle. When Jim left to get the order Colin spoke to the man. "Why don't you come over to the fire?" The man hesitated for a moment then sheepishly pulled up a chair alongside. When Jim brought the drinks he immediately lifted the glass and consumed it with one swallow. He sipped the second glass. "I'm not supposed to be in here. My daughter said she would sell the café if she found me in here. She would probably send me to that terrible psychiatric place."

"Tell me about it. My friend and I saw it when we were exploring."

He finished his second glass and the whisky made him more talkative.

"Yes it is a monstrosity of a place. It is an asylum. Some say that they have all been exposed to some kind of nerve gas that the government was experimenting with it on one of the islands. All the people in that building have all suffered." He poured some of the whisky out of his half bottle into a glass.

"I know that something is going on in that building. It's supposed to have been Sir Nigel Grant that built it. There was a lot of anger about it in the village. Putting such a building that the mothers send their children to the next village. A bus takes them back and forward."

He finished his drink, swaying as he made for the door. "A lot of secrets," he muttered. "A lot of secrets." Then he left the way he had come in, making sure that no one could see him leaving the pub. Colin sat after he had gone. There was something about the man that Colin felt sorry for. Maybe he was a bit of a drunk but there was something honest about him and he seemed to be afraid of something. When Jim came in from the bar Colin asked him. "Does he come in often?"

"No as a matter of fact this was only the second time."

Colin persisted. "What do you think he is afraid of?" Jim, not really interested, shrugged. "Probably that bad tempered daughter of his."

The next day he got a call from Carol. "You're not going to believe this Colin but I have been looking back at some of the history of Dunree. Nigel Grant's descendents were a pretty vicious lot. Going back a few hundred years to one Ralph Grant. He killed off half of the inhabitants of Dunree by poisoning their water supply. They died of typhoid but at the time the local magistrate couldn't prove it.

Apparently he did it because one of the local girls spurned his attention. The present Sir Nigel's great great grandfather fell out with one of the villagers. He got his henchmen to barricade the windows and doors leaving them trapped inside. Father, mother and three young children with no food or water. The villagers were afraid to release them.

Eventually some men from the next village rescued them. They were alive, just, but a few days afterwards the youngest child, a three year old died. Doesn't it seem unbelievable that one terrible man could cause such evil? But I suppose going back a few hundred years the man who owned their homes and their living had all the power.

Do you know Colin as I was reading the history of the village I could understand the fear that the name Grant aroused, even today."

"Don't worry my darling Colin. I will love you no matter what your name is. Do you know I have a feeling that Sir Nigel Grant knew you were a Grant when you entered Dunree. And wasn't it strange when you were injured on the hill he sent one of his men to help you and from what you told me he bent over backwards to help you with the orders from Sir Nigel himself. And yet anyone else who approaches the castle is chased away.

In the past four hundred years your father seemed to think that his ancestors came from the Dunree area. I'm sure there is a connection and you said that at one point visiting an old house that you got a strange feeling, and knowing to find the key above the door.

Someone climbing in the hills near the castle claimed that he heard a woman screaming. It was put down to the cry of an animal. Maybe a peacock.

I am missing you so much Colin. I would love to get another four days at Dunree but things are pretty hectic here at the station. A large quantity of drugs was found when a lorry was stopped quite close to Dunree. The driver denied all knowledge of their existence. He had driven from Croatia with this lorry with four old cars. They would be worked on to make them fit to drive then taken back to Croatia. The driver said that this went on all the time. Only in Britain could they get the parts for them."

"And now an investigation is going on and the driver is in custody. He said that he was told to drive into his usual yard and collect it back in a couple of days.

Something else I found out going through the old archives was a number of young girls in and around Dunree went missing and in spite of months of searching they were never found. Eventually it was presumed that they had just run off to the nearest town. A bit strange that over a few years so many young girls should decide to run away. I think that Dunree holds quite a lot of secrets."

Colin sat thinking after Carol's phone call. I don't want to leave here till I find some answers. If only to get it all put in place. To take home to his father the history of the Grants in the area.

He continued walking about the village. Usually it was deserted. Whether it was because they were getting used to seeing him but quite a few people started to appear from their little cottages. They didn't speak, just hurried past, heads bent. Good heavens he thought. This village seems to have gone back a hundred years. He ventured back to the little café. Nothing had changed. The same unpleasant girl still stood behind the counter. She glared at him, putting down the magazine she had been reading. "Yes what do you want?" He asked for a coffee. She switched on the kettle and produced a jar of instant coffee. "Do you want sugar?" He shook his head. "Well there isn't any milk. He never left any this morning. I suppose it's because he hasn't been paid."

For some reason Colin felt sorry for her. What an existence for a young girl. She was probably wishing that she could leave the village but not able to leave her father. He would not survive on his own. She was more or less a prisoner.

On his way back to the inn he passed a crowd of people gathered in the village square. There seemed to be some sort of service going on being led by the Salvation Army. He stood at the back of the crowd. He noticed that some of the women were weeping.

A hymn was sung led by the Salvation Army. He asked an old man standing beside him what the service was about. He just looked at him for a moment as if deciding whether to speak. Then in his soft highland voice he explained the service was for a young girl who had disappeared exactly a year ago from the village. The service was asking for her safe return.

The old man shook his head. I think the lass has gone to join all the other girls who disappeared over the years from this village. One by one the crowd returned to their homes. There was no conversation between them which in itself was unusual.

Colin remembered the telephone call he had had from Carol telling him about the girls who had gone missing over the years from the village and here was another only a year ago. Colin felt a shiver going through him. It was too much of a coincidence that they should all have disappeared to go into the towns and he also felt that the people of Dunree felt the same as him.

Back at the inn a few more people had arrived but only for one night, just passing through on their way to Glasgow or Edinburgh.

The four men were seated at their usual table when Colin went into the bar at night. He realised that he hadn't paid much attention to what they looked like. It was only their strange behaviour that had drawn his attention. Now he studied them more closely. They were all about the same age. He was surprised to notice that they were much younger. They were, he guessed, maybe between thirty and thirty five. They were all about six foot, broad shouldered and strong looking. All had the same lifeless look about them apart from being deaf and dumb. They seemed to be drugged. He looked at their hands. They were the hands of manual workers. Then he remembered that that was what they were. Digging in the garden at the asylum. Colin had a thought. What if they decided not to sit quietly like zombies? He certainly would not like to be in the same room as them. In the few days that he had been here in Dunree one thing after another was a puzzle to him. And one of the biggest puzzles that he had stumbled upon on his first day in the mountains.

Chapter 6

The next morning after a quick breakfast he decided to walk again on the mountain. He just seemed to be drawn to it. Jim made him up a packed lunch. "Which part are you making for? It is the rule you know to say whereabouts on the mountain you are heading. One never knows when someone is on their own an accident could happen and it helps the mountain rescue if they know which area to search. Mind you, you already have had the experience and you were lucky to be found."

"Well," Colin considered. "I think maybe I'll go round the opposite side away from the Grant's mansion. With all the stories I have heard I think I would be wise to stay well clear."

It was a beautiful morning. Quite a heat in the sun but there was still a few patches of snow. After a few hours walking he decided to sit and have lunch. He sat on a large stone and looked around. The view was breathtaking. In the distance was the village surrounded by mountains and in the far away distance a touch of blue.

"Why that's a loch." He took out his map to look for it. A sudden mountain breeze blew the map from his hand. It blew quite a bit before it landed on a patch of snow. He bent to pick it up and noticed strange marks. They looked like tyre marks. But that's impossible. How could a car travel in this part of the mountain with all the rocks scattered around? And it must be nearly three thousand feet high.

He packed away his map and lunch things and decided to follow the tracks. They seemed to go through some rough parts. A lot of scree from the top of the mountain didn't seem to bother whatever the vehicle was.

He started to get tired and was thinking about giving up when just in front of him were large iron gates. The sort of gates one would see maybe outside a factory. But what took his breath away was at the end of a long wide driveway was Sir Nigel Grant's mansion.

He just stood. He couldn't believe what he was seeing, that this was where the strange tracks led to. He heard the sound of a motor starting up. He stepped back behind the gate and he saw the strangest looking vehicle. It was something like a snow mobile but at least three times bigger.

As he watched the wheels lifted up and it looked like a hovercraft with a sort of cushion of air replacing them. So that was how it managed over the rough ground Colin thought. But where had it come from was his next thought. This mountain gets more and more mysterious.

He suddenly realized that he had better get away before he was discovered spying. He got off the mountain as quickly as possible. He decided not to mention anything to anyone, not even to Carol.

When he arrived back at the inn there was a lot of activity going on. A large van was in the car park. He saw two uniformed police standing beside it. A man and women came out of the van, the man in plain clothes, the woman in uniform. Then his heart gave a leap. The woman was Carol. He almost ran towards them.

Carol in uniform was such a surprise. If anything she looked more beautiful. It was such a strange feeling looking at her and realising that she really was a policewoman. Colin longed to take her in his arms but she just gave him her lovely smile and introduced him to the man.

"Colin this is James. He is in charge. We are here investigating what we think might be a drugs run heading for Glasgow." She turned to James who was looking a bit puzzled. "Colin is a very special friend of mine." James grinned at her. "Of course. This is the special friend from New Zealand." Carol blushed. "So you knew all along?" "Of course," he said. "I am a policeman you know." Colin liked him. For someone with his rank he had a sort of fatherly attitude but there was sharpness about his eyes.

"I'll be staying in the inn. The others will be in the van but we will all meet for dinner," Carol explained. She turned back to James. "Colin and I have been puzzling about some of the things that are going on here. Apart from the drug investigation we might find out just what is going on."

That night the three of them sat down to dinner. The conversation was all about the village. "Well," James said. "What you are saying I believe. But remember," he turned to Carol. "We have a job to do and we can't be sidetracked on to something else." He refused their invitation to join them for a drink in the bar. "I must head off to the van and catch up on some notes. I will meet you at breakfast and immediately after we can start some enquiries round the village."

Colin realised that in the nicest way he was put in his place to let them get on with their police work. He went with Carol to the bar. "I'll just have one drink," she said. "I must keep a clear head because I know what will happen tomorrow. James is a stickler for getting a job done. We will probably be working throughout the day interviewing the village to try to find out if anybody had heard any whispers about drugs."

The same old scene welcomed them in the bar. The only difference was a fifth man had joined the usual four. He appeared to be much younger than them but like the rest there was no conversation and when the Keeper came in the five of them stood up and went out with him.

"Right," Colin said. "Enough is enough. Tomorrow night I am going to leave before them and hide next door in the doorway." Carol looked worried. "I don't think that's a good idea Colin. What if the Keeper spots you? And those men look as if they could break your body in two." He gave her a hug. "OK don't worry. Let's just enjoy our drink and what about a short stroll about the village. It's a beautiful night.

They walked to the end of the road arms round each other. Carol looked around. "It really is a beautiful village." As she spoke the moon rose from behind the mountains bathing the village in its light. "Oh Colin," she whispered. "I will never forget tonight. It's as if the whole world belongs to us." They headed back to the inn. At the foot of the stairs they clung together, neither of them wanting to part. Carol pulled away. "I will see you at breakfast," and with a swift kiss she ran up the stairs.

It so happened that Colin, after a sleepless night, was late going down to breakfast. Carol and James had already gone. He spent most of the day not quite knowing what to do with himself. He decided to have a walk round the village. His steps took him to the little café. He was just in time to see the girl leaving. She was heading towards the bus stop. The sign said the café was open. Curiosity took him in.

He was the only customer. He was surprised to see that it was the girl's father who was working and he seemed to be quite sober. When he saw Colin he looked embarrassed. For a moment he looked as if he would ignore him just calling across the room asking if he could help him. Colin ordered a coffee and when he brought it to the table he turned away. Colin caught his arm. "How are you today?" He gave a sigh and pulled out a chair. "I am sorry if I was a nuisance the other night in the inn. Forget that I was there. I haven't had a drink since. My daughter, for the first time in weeks, was able to leave me in charge."

"I certainly won't discuss you but I must admit that the conversation we had I found very interesting. Could we maybe have a talk another time?" "No no, definitely not." He got up quickly. "You are welcome to the coffee." He disappeared into the back and he didn't appear again. Colin finished his coffee and walking past the café on his way back he noticed that once again he was behind the counter.

After dinner James went off to the van leaving them to go into the pub. Carol looked quite shattered. "Oh boy Colin. It's part of the job that I find so boring. Interviewing the village residents. Nobody has ever seen anything.

Mind you one old man out of the dozens we interviewed told us that he had seen a big car transporter two or three times. He explained that he spent most of the night awake usually getting up in the early hours to make himself a cup of tea. It was the loud noise of the big lorry that drew him to the window. It really was a breakthrough. It meant that what the driver we had in custody had said about taking the wrong road did not seem plausible."

"Let's forget about it all," Carol said. "And go for a stroll.

"Two things I have been thinking about Carol are it not a bit unusual for you to call your superior officer James." Carol laughed. "Oh Colin. That is true. Normally I would call him Sir but because of the nature of our enquiries it is better to be casual to get the villagers to relax."

Chapter 7

"And what other thoughts did you have my darling Colin?" "Well really not that important," he said. "I think I know what it was," Carol laughed. "You were wondering when we are going to manage to have sex. And the answer to that my darling. I don't know. When I am wearing this uniform and working on a case I have to be discreet. I would lose respect from the old inhabitants if I have to interview them."

Colin pulled her into his arms and hugged her. They melted into each other's arms. Her lips were so soft and enticing but they drew apart, aware that they were probably being watched from behind the curtains.

Jim greeted them when they went in. "I have had a phone call from Kevin. He booked rooms for tomorrow night. He will arrive quite late because he will be travelling by bus. His sister Sally will be driving here. He wanted to get more skiing in."

Colin turned to Carol. "A smashing young American couple. You will like them. They did say they would be back to spend a few more days here before flying back to America. We will probably all meet in the pub."

The next day as usual Carol and James left immediately after breakfast. They had more interviewing to do. Colin, at a loose end, helped Jim in the cellar moving the crates about. He pulled at an iron bar that was sticking out of the wall. "A bit dangerous that Jim. I nearly tripped over it." Colin examined it. It was about two feet long.

He took it closer to the light. There was some letters on the flat bit at the end. "Why it looks like a branding iron." "Let me have a look." Jim rubbed the letters with a bit of rag. He gasped. He looked at Colin and handed it to him. The letters spelled witch. "You were right Colin it is a branding iron." They looked at each other in horror. Jim dropped it and stepped back. "How on earth did it come in here? It must have been used on some poor soul accused of being a witch." Colin, much calmer, tried to get Jim calmed down.

"Look Jim it's got nothing to do with you. You just happened to buy this inn which is, as you know, a few hundred years old. And anyway maybe it was never used."

"But why make such a horrible thing?" Jim wasn't convinced and in his own mind Colin doubted it himself. "Come on Jim let's go back up to the bar and forget about it. We mustn't tell anyone. If the local people heard about it they wouldn't come near the inn. You know as well as me how superstitious the highland people can be. And goodness only knows there seems to be enough mystery going on here."

Colin went up to his bedroom to have a shower. He just felt that he wanted to get rid of the feeling that he had got in the cellar. And besides he had to freshen up. Carol and Jimmy would be arriving soon. It would be interesting to find out how they had got on with their enquiries. He met them as they came in. It had been a long day for them. Carol once again looked tired. She rushed upstairs to have a shower.

And later when they were sitting having dinner James spoke about another day of little help. "Tomorrow I think you should have a day off Carol. I have got to go to Glasgow to check up on a few things. One thing in particular, I want to find out a bit about that asylum before we visit it."

There were five men at the table when he went into the bar with Carol. He was feeling pretty tense thinking about what was in the cellar. He knew that he was being stupid. It could have been there for hundreds of years.

When Carol left to go upstairs he made a decision. Before the Keeper arrived to take them away he went out and concealed himself where he could get a good view of them when they left the pub. It was only a few minutes afterwards that a van appeared and stopped near the door of the inn. The keeper was the driver. He went in and appeared back with the five men.

He opened the back door of the van and more or less shoved them in. Colin was expecting the van to take the road to the asylum but instead it drove towards the Keeper's cottage. Colin raced after it. He was just in time to see the Keeper bundling them into his house. He crept to a window. He only got a quick glance inside before the curtains were drawn. The men were putting on what looked like long surgeons gowns. Good heavens. It looked as if they were going to do an operation.

Colin just stood. He couldn't move. Just what the hell was going on? Even as he stood the light was switched off. The whole house was in darkness.

He tried to find himself a reason. Maybe it was just night wear that the men had put on and now they had all gone to bed. Otherwise why switch off the light. But why all sleep at the Keeper's. All the questions were going round in his head. There was no answer to it all.

The next morning Carol suggested that they spend the day on the mountain. "Just what I need," Colin agreed. As usual Jim made them a packed lunch. The day was beautiful. Spring was bursting out all around. The trees were in bud just waiting on nature's call to spring into leaf. Once or twice they frightened a bird, almost stepping on them as they nestled in the heather.

"Tell me about your life," Colin asked Carol. "Well," she said. "Not a great deal of excitement in my life. I have a young brother Allister. He is sixteen, mad on football and my sister Rachel who is eighteen. She is at Strathclyde. My dad recently retired from the police. The police was his life. He was well known in our area and I think he was respected. I think that it was from him I always wanted to follow in his footsteps." "And a jolly good police woman you are."

"Now what about you Colin Grant. What about your family a few hundred years ago."

"Oh don't talk about it. It's awful to think that one family over the generations can blacken a family name." "Don't worry Colin. It's only in this small village that the Grant name is taboo because the villagers did suffer and the stories get passed from generation to generation." Colin silenced her by holding her pressed against him and kissing her till she was breathless. "Let's go home past the asylum and see what's happening there."

Carol looked at him, a dubious expression on her face. "Are you sure Colin? It seems to me that the strange happenings in the village are becoming an obsession with you." "Anyway let's just do it and see if the men are still around." "Tomorrow when James comes back we are going to talk to whoever is in charge."

As they approached the asylum they could hear the sound of men working and when they looked in the gate there they were as usual. They seemed to be building a wall. There was no sign of the Keeper.

Arriving back at the inn they found Kevin had just arrived. Colin looked round. "And where is Sally?" Kevin frowned. "Well that's something I would like to know. She set off from Aviemore early this morning. I thought she would be here but knowing my sister she may have spotted something of interest on the way."

Dinner time approached and still there was no sign of her. They all started to worry. "Maybe the car has broken down. There are long stretches of road where there is no help for any motorist. They just have to rely on the help of a passing motorist," Jim said. "But she does have a mobile phone. Why has she not used it?"

Kevin was getting more and more upset. "Look," Jim said. "I'll take the car. We will travel along the road she would have taken." "We will all go with you," Colin suggested. But Jim shook his head. "No only you Kevin. Someone must stay here in case she rings." It was fortunate that there were no more guests in the inn. Carol shook her head. "I don't like this Colin. A young girl in a strange country going missing."

"Well maybe there is no cause for concern. Her car could have broken down and remember that there are some places among the hills where the phone doesn't work. Come on let's go and sit in the lounge. I don't fancy going in the bar and looking at those strange men night after night."

"What do you mean Colin? Why do you call them strange?" "Oh Carol. Ever the policeman." Colin was silent for a few minutes. Making up his mind he decided to tell her about what had happened when he decided to spy on the men and the Keeper. Carol was listening and looking at him. "I am so angry with you Colin. What on earth possessed you to do something so foolish if not dangerous? What if they saw you spying on them? What excuse could you have made? From what you tell me it seems to be innocent enough. So the men spent the night at the Keeper's?"

As she spoke Colin felt a bit foolish. She was right. "I think that it is the atmosphere in this village that is getting to me." They heard the sound of a car stopping at the door and Jim's voice. They went to meet them hoping that Sally was with them but it was only Kevin and Jim. Jim ushered them back into the lounge. Kevin was as white as a sheet, his whole body shaking. Jim told them that just a few miles from the end of the village they found Sally's car. No sign of her. Kevin's bags were in the car but Sally's bags were missing.

"What about the car?" Carol asked. "Had it broken down?" "No the car was fine," Jim said. "I started it up. It went fine and there was plenty of petrol. No reason for her stopping unless of course she pulled in to do the toilet and fell into a ditch. We were going to drive the car back here but I thought it was better to leave it to pin point where to search as soon as it was light. I've already phoned the police. They too will wait till morning. There was no point in moving about in the dark."

"That's true," Carol said. "They will want to follow any footprints of Sally's. A lot of people moving about could be confusing." They all sat glumly. None of them wanted to go to bed. Jim brought in some drinks. "I just don't understand," Kevin kept saying. "She should have been here hours ago. And why did she take her bags from the car? My bags were there because I was travelling by bus. It was easier for Sally to take them with her in the car. Oh God what has happened to her? We just had two days left before flying back home."

Jim and Carol went to the kitchen to make sandwiches and heat up some soup. Nobody had had dinner and it was going to be a long night. Nobody was talking. Each one was afraid to say the wrong thing, all just waiting for dawn to get out and start searching. This couldn't be a case of a young teenager wanting to leave the village for the city as only one year ago it was presumed that that was what had happened to the young girl who had gone missing.

The drugs case was put to the side. Carol and James were put in charge of the search for Sally because they had been familiarised with the area. Into the second day more police were drafted in. locals were encouraged to help in the search. Kevin was absolutely distraught. He blamed himself for letting Sally drive from Aviemore on her own.

He kept hoping hour by hour that she would be found. He was preparing himself to phone his mum and dad to tell them that Sally was missing. The inn was closed. The police had asked Jim if they could use the inn as a base. In no time the lounge was set up with phones and a large screen, Sally's photo in the centre with all the details. TV sets about the room focused on the moorland round where the car was found. The phone kept ringing. People had spotted Sally when she had stopped at a wayside coffee bar five miles from Dunree. It helped narrow the search to within a mile from the car. What reason could she have had to pull into the side of the road so close to Dunree.

Into the third day the police believed that she had been stopped, waved down by someone. Kevin was asked again and again if Sally had met someone at Aviemore and arranged to meet them. It was just clutching at straws. Neither the police nor Kevin believed it. They just kept going over every possibility.

Chapter 8

It was now four days since Sally disappeared. The search was still concentrated round the car area. There wasn't even footprints that they could follow because all round the area was solid hard scree from the mountain all frozen solid from the recent frosts.

Kevin's mum and dad had phoned to say they would be arriving the next day. They were going to fly to Heathrow and then get a flight to Glasgow. Jim volunteered to take his car to meet them. It gave Kevin something else to think about. He was happy that Jim would be with him. And so it went on. Each one trying to give each other support.

At one point Colin turned to Carol. "I wonder what is happening to the Keeper and the men. They must be missing going to the pub for their beer." Carol looked at him. "You know we were going to visit the asylum to interview whoever is in charge before Sally went missing to see if they could shed any light on the drag lorry. After all it wasn't far from the asylum that it was found. Almost the same spot that Sally's car was found. I think I'll run this past James though knowing him I bet that he had already thought about it." The next morning Jim and Kevin set off early for Glasgow. Colin was at a loose end. Carol was busy with the team. He went to the kitchen to make a pile of sandwiches. Anything to keep his mind off what could have happened to Sally.

He brought them into the lounge to where they were all gathered round the large board. They were grateful for the short break. Some of them had been up all night. Maybe today there will be good news. Colin's heart went out to the parents. But things were not looking good. He put on his coat and went outside. Everything was so still. He walked to the end of the street thinking about all the strange things that had happened in such a short space of time. He went to sit on one of the benches but it was already occupied.

He thought it was a tramp all wrapped up with what looked like a blanket round his shoulders. He went to walk away when a voice came out of the bundle of clothes. He recognised the voice. "Sit by me," he said. It was the old man that had spoken to him on the day of remembrance for the young girl who had gone missing.

Colin sat down. "Why are you sitting here?" he asked him. "It's a bit too chilly to be out so early." "I'm just fine. I told you before. I just can't sleep. I am happier sitting here. I could tell you some strange stories. Oh yes nothing has changed here for hundreds of years." Colin wasn't paying him much attention. Just the ramblings of an old man. Then he heard him saying something about the Grants. "What was that?" Colin asked him. The old man peered at him from behind his blanket. "Well it's happening again," he muttered. "It's happening again."

"What do you mean it's happening again?" Colin thought he better humour the old man. "What I say," he muttered. "Old Joe isn't as stupid as some would like to think." He clutched Colin's arm. "One year ago a young girl went missing. Now there is another. Three years ago another village girl disappeared. Oh yes supposed to have run away to the town. I know that's wrong. They were happy living here. My granddaughter Jenny was the girl who went missing. Three years ago she was sixteen and she loved the village and the mountains. My daughter has never given up looking for her. She was an only child. Her father died a few years before she went missing."

As Colin looked at the old man he saw the tears running down his cheeks. "Come now Joe I'll take you home." Colin helped him to his feet. A woman came running from one of the little cottages. "Oh dad you will be the death of me, wandering off in the middle of the night."

"This is Colin Grant." The woman stepped back away from them. "Now now Kathy. Colin is from New Zealand. He has got nothing to do with the village. He is a friend. He listens when I talk to him." He turned to Colin. "My daughter Kathy. It was her daughter Jenny who went missing."

Colin was impressed at the way Joe made the introductions. Suddenly he wasn't just an old tramp like man. There was such a lot of gentleman's pride in him and Colin thought good manners were inherited in the Scottish Highlanders.

He turned to Colin. "Maybe tomorrow if it's a fine day you might take a wander to the seat. I have a story to tell you." He said something Colin didn't understand. He found out later it was Gaelic. He had said God be with you.

Colin found it hard meeting Kevin's parents. To see the heartbreak in their faces but trying to be brave for each other. "We had a discussion in the car coming here. We are going to try and rent a house in or near the village. We think it will be easier. Kevin agrees. He will of course stay with us. We will try to get something tomorrow."

As it happened Jim knew of a small cottage in the village which was rented out in the summer months. He would talk to the owners.

Colin managed to get some time alone with Carol. They walked outside. "How are things going," Colin asked. Carol shook her head. "There is nothing, absolutely nothing. Not even one clue to help us. Already the force has started to release some of the men back to their duties in Glasgow. I suspect that Sally will be joining all the other girls who have gone missing from Dunree over the years. They will join the files missing persons. Oh Colin what is it with this village."

Jim was talking to James. "He says that he has had enough. He is putting the inn up for sale. He isn't worried about making a loss if he can get a quick sale."

Carol and James decided to break off from Sally's search to continue interviewing more of the residents just to see if they could give them anything else about drugs that may have been passing through their village.

They decided to go to the asylum. When they pulled the bell at the large gate the usual four men just continued working. The Keeper came to the gate. "What do you want? Nobody is allowed in here. James showed him his badge. "And this is my inspector. Take us to whoever is in charge.

The Keeper grudgingly opened the gate. They followed him to what seemed to be a reception area. It seemed just like a prison. Bare stone walls and floor. The Keeper took them to one of the doors and led them down a long corridor with doors all the way along. At the end he knocked at one of them and a voice asked who it was.

The Keeper replied "It's the police." There was silence for a few moments. They were told to go in. The room was in complete contrast to what they had seen outside. A thick green carpet covered the floor. Long velvet curtains the same colour covered large windows. One wall was covered in bookcases. A large desk was near one of the windows. The man sitting behind it was difficult to describe. His hair was pure white which gave him a look of age but his face was that of a younger man. When he stood up Carol thought he must be over six feet.

"I am Ronald Grant McLean. He stretched out his hand. What can I do to help you?" His voice was soft, almost gentle. Unexpected for someone so tall. James explained the reason for their visit.

"Well I really can't do much to help you. Certainly we do have a certain amount of drugs here as you will understand. They are absolutely necessary for the patients. If you wish someone will take you to our dispensary. Books are kept there of all the drugs."

"Thank you," James said. "Now could you tell me who owns this establishment and who are the men who visit the pub each evening." Carol marvelled at the neat way James had slipped in the questions.

"Sir Nigel Grant built the asylum and runs it with his own money. Most of the men in here are ex army. The four men you mentioned are, as you probably know, deaf and dumb and also have some brain damage.

It was the result of an experiment with some kind of nerve gas in a very secret location.

The four men you talk about are doctors and scientists but they are like children and after a hard day's work they look forward to the treat of a pint in the bar. They are very gentle but Keeper watches over them." He put his hand in the air. "One never knows." He rang a bell. A man came in. "He is in charge of the dispensary. He will show you around. I hope I have been of some help to you." They followed Angus from the room.

The dispensary was kept in pristine order. Angus pointed out the cabinets with all the drugs. Each cabinet was marked stating which one was used for a particular diagnosis. Each cabinet was locked. Angus showed them the bunch of keys strapped at his waist. "I am the only one who has access."

James thanked him and made to open the door. Angus moved quickly and opened the door for them. When they went out James said. "Well that was a waste of time apart from Mr. Ronald Grant McLean. I would like to find out a bit more about him. You have gone very quiet Carol."

"Well James I am just trying to work out why the cabinet behind the door had a shelf with packets of Tampax in it. Especially in an all male establishment."

"Well you amaze me Carol. That was well spotted."

"In fact is Angus jumping in front of it that drew my attention? Remember how quick he was to open the door.

"Well that settles it," James said. "I will get a search warrant for the place."

Back at the inn there was still nothing in the search for Sally. Kevin had moved in with his mum and dad. Carol was pleased that they were together. Kevin had his parents. They could share their grief away from the crowds at the inn. There wasn't as many. Tomorrow would be the sixth day since she had gone missing. A lot of the volunteer searchers had got things in their own lives to get on with.

With all that was going on Colin had forgotten about the old man he had promised to meet. He made his way there after breakfast. He found him sitting on the seat with the same blanket round him. "How are you today?" Colin asked.

Joe looked at him. "I have been waiting to talk to you since yesterday. You said you would meet me."

Colin looked at the poor old man. His lip was trembling. He was just like a child who had been deprived of something. "I'm sorry Joe. The missing girl's parents arrived from America. Jim went to Glasgow to meet them and I was looking after the inn. Now Joe what story did you say you would tell me."

He pulled the blanket lightly round his shoulders and looked at Colin with bright bird like eyes. "I'm just a silly old man. You will be thinking that maybe I'm not right in the head. But you know old people like me get upset very easy but my memory is good. What I'm going to tell you has been passed down from my ancestors. The Grants were trouble in their day. And they are trouble today.

The past is never really past. Something is brought forward from generation to generation. The good and the bad things in people come out. You have a girlfriend. I have seen you walking with her. She is a lovely girl. I think you love her." Colin nodded.

"Well what I'm going to tell you is the result of love turning into an obsession of hate and fear. A hundred years ago an ancestor of the present Sir Nigel built this village and the present house on the mountain. It was said he built it to look down on the village and the village people that he more or less owned because if they were dissatisfied and complained they would be turned out of their homes.

One couple had a small cottage high up on the hill. He was a shepherd. They had a daughter. She never went to the village school but sometimes the governess at the big house who was there to teach the son, the only child they had, would make a point of visiting the shepherd's cottage to give the child some schooling. As the years passed the mother died at an early age. The father, broken hearted, died the year after. Lucy their daughter was just fifteen.

The factor came from the big house to turn her out to put a man in to look after the sheep. Lucy persuaded him to let her stay. She knew as much about shepherding as her father. When she was sixteen she got a horse to help her gather the sheep for sales that take place twice a year. It was kept in a lean to beside the house. Lucy loved it. Another year passed. At seventeen she blossomed into a real beauty galloping over the hills, her hair the colour of corn, flying out behind her. She would visit the village occasionally to get supplies but mostly she kept to herself."

Joe went quiet. Colin realised that the poor old man was exhausting himself but he was desperate to hear the rest of the story. They both sat quietly for a while then Joe started to talk again.

"It was one day when she was gathering the sheep near the big house when Nigel Grant spotted her. There she was a beautiful young woman and he wanted her. And with all his wealth what he wanted he got. He talked to her in his charming way. Oh yes," Joe continued. "He could be charming and in fact for his age he was quite a handsome man. Day after day he made a point of running into her wherever she was. Lucy the innocent girl just accepted him for what he was, her boss. Eventually he found his way into her cottage bringing her little gifts. He was becoming totally obsessed with her.

Late in the summer Lucy working as usual took the horse to a little burn to drink. She lay down. With the heat of the day she dozed off. A voice woke her. "What have we here? A little shepherdess lying asleep while the sheep stray." She jumped to her feet. There was a young man looking down at her from his horse. He was laughing at her. "Don't you remember me Lucy?" She looked at him. He was very handsome she thought with his fair hair and brilliant blue eyes. There was a haughty air about him, the way he sat on his horse.

Then suddenly she recognised him. It was Mark Grant the son of the big house. She hadn't seen him since they were children sharing their schooling before he was sent away to boarding school. Lucy suddenly felt shy before him. When they were children it didn't matter that he belonged to the big house and she was a shepherd's daughter. He really was handsome. She felt a fluttering in her heart. The feeling felt so strange. She had had very little contact with boys or for that matter any children her own age."

"Will you excuse me Sir? I must get on with my work. If the sheep stray the factor will be angry with me." He laughed at her. "Now Lucy. Why the Sir? You always knew me as Mark." He came down off the horse. "Come Lucy. Tell me what has been happening to you." He was so relaxed that Lucy started to feel relaxed with him. They spoke for a while then Mark climbed back on his horse. But before he left he said. "I think that maybe tomorrow I will come and help you with the sheep."

And true to his word he suddenly appeared. He was carrying a picnic basket. "Look," he said to her. "I have brought lunch." And so every few days he would appear. She asked him once if his father would approve of him being in her company such a lot. And his reply had been. "My father and I don't have a lot in common. We don't have a lot of conversations at dinner. The only time we share he doesn't even ask what I have been doing during the day." But he was wrong. His father was very interested.

Colin climbed higher and higher. All the tension that he had been feeling the last few days just disappeared. Then high in the sky a speck appeared. As it got closer he saw that it was a light aircraft. It must be Mark. I would love to talk to him. Maybe before I go away back home. Then he felt the feeling of peace disappear. He would have to go back to New Zealand. His parents were putting pressure on him to come home and maybe start working in a practice. He owed it to them. They had sacrificed so much for him to become a doctor.

Life was certainly strange. He had the feeling that his father had in some way manipulated him to come to Dunree to trace ancestors. It was all a bit confusing and once again he thought about the writing in the

Church. Was he the one that was ordained to purify the village of the atrocities of the Grants? But then he himself was a Grant. His father had taught him to be proud of the name Grant and the motto Stand Fast.

Well maybe that's what I will do. Stand fast and clear the village of the evil that is lurking there. He turned back to the inn feeling happy the decision had been made.

I think that if it was someone else Joe would just clam up. I think he is telling me the story because of my name.

Already he was having second thoughts. Maybe he shouldn't have told Carol. She was police and she was trained to get to the bottom of anything. He just hoped she wouldn't try to get the rest of the story out of Joe.

The next morning in spite of a hangover he couldn't wait to go to meet Joe to get the rest of the story. He arrived at the seat. There was no sign of Joe. He hung about for nearly an hour. He didn't put in an appearance. He was just plucking up courage to go to his house when his daughter appeared. "I was watching you hanging about waiting for my father. Well he won't be coming. He isn't well thanks to you. He stayed out too long in the cold talking to you."

Colin apologised to her and indeed he felt guilty. He had been so taken up with his story he hadn't noticed that the poor old man was getting cold. And I call myself a doctor. He knew that with someone Joe's age a cold could be fatal.

He made his way back to the inn. Jim was busy cleaning in the bar. He shouted to Colin. "Could you do me a favour? I need to go to the cellar. I'm running out of beer. Could you give me a hand?" Colin smiled to himself. He knew that Jim didn't want to go alone. He was a bit scared of the cellar.

Colin patted him on the back. "Poor old Jim. You will have to face going to the cellar alone. There is nothing there to be afraid of. Let's go and get rid of that branding iron if it will make you feel better." Colin went to the corner where he had come across the branding iron. There was nothing there. They started to search every nook and cranny. No sign of it.

"Jim did you have anyone coming down here?" "No definitely not. I have the keys on a ring along with all the other keys. I take them with me all the time. They are clipped on to my belt because when I first came here I kept losing them."

Suddenly Jim stopped talking. He was looking at the hatch. "Someone has been in here. Look the hatch isn't shut properly." Colin looked. Jim was right. It was open just a crack. The padlock was hanging off at the side. Someone had been desperate to get in.

"What is that hatch there for?" Colin asked. Jim was visibly upset. "It's used by the brewers but they haven't been for months and when they come I have to open the hatch for them." They stood looking at each other. Why would someone break in? Jim looked at the crates. They hadn't been touched.

One thought was in both their minds. They came to get the branding iron. Colin felt an icy shiver going down his spine. "Let's get what we came for and get to hell out of here."

They were both a bit shaken. They sat in the bar. Each had a large whisky. "I think we should report it to the police. After all it was a break in." "Oh I don't know Jim." Colin tried to put him off but he was determined. "OK", Colin decided. "Tell the police about the break in but don't mention the branding iron to them. Goodness knows what will get stirred up." After some more thought Jim agreed.

When Carol and James arrived at night Jim told them. At once they both went to the cellar to examine the hatch. When they appeared back James spoke to Jim. "Do you realise that whoever broke in could have access to the whole place? The door into the cellar had such a flimsy lock it could easily be knocked in from the cellar side. And you can't be too careful because after all you are responsible for the guests." Neither of them had thought about that. Jim accepted the ticking off from James. "It will get fixed tomorrow," he promised.

Later Carol asked Colin what he thought about the break in. "It seems a bit strange to both James and I. Nothing was stolen. We think that whoever did it was looking for something. Is James sure that there was nothing stolen?" "Well maybe they were disturbed before they got in." He felt awful lying to Carol.

Carol and James were now working from the Port-a-cabin and caravan. They were going to visit the asylum again but this time they had a search warrant. Looking for Susan was still a priority. They were talking about the mum and dad making an appeal on television. The thoughts now seemed to be going towards her being in Glasgow or Edinburgh. She could have been abducted when she was stopped for some reason in the lay by.

Colin was unsettled. He knew that he should be making plans to go home to New Zealand. He decided on the spur of the moment to go back to the house on the mountain. He was sure that that was the house that Joe was talking about. He went to find Jim to tell him where he was going and to get some sandwiches. Jim was worried. "Don't do anything rash. There is enough happening here without you getting into trouble."

It was a beautiful spring day. So different from the day he first came on the house with the snow thick on the ground. He came on a track that he hadn't noticed but it would have been covered in snow. He just turned round from the burn and there it was. Once again he got a strange feeling.

Nothing seemed to have changed except there was no ladder. Someone must have finished the work they were doing. He walked slowly up to the house. He looked at what could be called a lean-to but it had no roof. It looked ready to fall down. He was sure that was where she kept her horse.

He tried to look in the window but it was so covered in dirt that he couldn't see a thing. He realised that he was putting off the moment when he would see if the key was still in the same place above the door. He put his hand in and there it was. He put it in the door. It turned quite easily which surprised him.

Then he was in the room. After the sun outside it seemed dark inside. Once again he wanted to get out. He looked around. The fireplace in one wall with an iron pot all rusted. At the side a table with two or three wooden chairs. There was a large cupboard. He opened the door. There were the usual utensils and on one shelf there were a number of stone jars.

He opened a lid and there still remained the faintest smell of some kind of herb. Each jar contained a different herb. Because they were in sealed stone jars they looked as if they could still be used. At the side of the fire place was a large iron bed. The mattress had long rotted away but there was dried bracken and what he thought was some more herbs still lying in it.

He suddenly felt quite sad. This was where the young girl had lain. Suddenly he wanted to find out everything about the girl. He went out and locked the door putting the key back above the door. He wanted to talk to Joe again to hear the rest of his story. He had a strange feeling that he was supposed to go to Dunree and that for some reason he was to find the house that a young girl had lived in.

When he talked to Carol that night he didn't mention visiting the house on the hill. He couldn't understand why he was loath to talk to anyone about it.

Carol was in a happy mood. She had the next day off. Surprise, surprise. She said to Colin. "I have arranged to get a car and I am going to show you some of the sights of the Highlands. All you seem to have seen is the city and this village and I think it is beginning to get us both down. So what do you think Colin?" Colin hugged her. "I think you are a very clever girl."

The rain woke him in the morning. It was coming down in buckets. Oh well, so much for our trip out. He turned round and went back to sleep.

A hammering on the door woke him after about an hour. Carol was shouting. "Come on lazy bones I'm ready to go." "But it's raining," he shouted back. "Come on. The forecast is good for the afternoon."

They set off, Carol carrying a large hamper." Just in case we get lost in the middle of the mountains."

Colin was amazed and excited. "It's all absolutely breathtaking." He took photo after photo. "You are going to set that camera on fire."

The forecast was right. The sun did come out just as they entered the valley of Glencoe. "Now," Carol said to him. "There are plenty of mountains for you." It was unbelievably beautiful. The sun shone on the waterfalls turning them into liquid silver. "Oh I wish my parents could see this. There is something so special about it," Colin said

Chapter 9

They parked in a lay-by looking down the valley. "Well Colin I had a reason for bringing you to Glencoe. Remember you were a bit doubtful about the story Joe told you about Dunree going back over three hundred years. And how a story passed down for so many years could be true.

Well Colin the story of the Glencoe massacre happened just over three hundred years ago and people do still talk about it and every year one of the descendants lays a wreath on the anniversary. There is a monument in the village. I will take you to see it. I know that the circumstances between Dunree and Glencoe are entirely different but what I am saying is that what Joe told you apart from maybe a few details was correct."

"So what did happen hear Carol?" "Well to paraphrase it two clans, the MacDonalds of Glencoe and the Campbells were lifelong enemies. And King William of Orange wanted to make an example of what he called the rogue clan who would not sign the document of allegiance.

Anyway the MacDonalds chief decided at the last moment to sign. He was too late so an army was sent into Glencoe to punish them. The story that is told is that the regiment was made up mostly of Campbells. The regiment was billeted in and around Glencoe for nearly two weeks. Then one night without any warning they set about the massacre of all the inhabitants."

"Some escaped into the hills but it was the month of February 1692. The glen was covered in snow with a cold north east wind. Some died of the cold. The terrible thing about the massacre was that the MacDonalds had fed and entertained the Campbells for two weeks. Sometimes

Glencoe is called the glen of weeping and if you were to see it on a cold winter's day it lives up to that reputation.

Well Colin when we get back you must try to get Joe to finish the story of Dunree and I think that even although the story was handed down for generations, like the story of the massacre, Joe's story is probably all true."

Arriving back at the inn there was great excitement. A woman fitting Sally's description was found wandering on the street in Edinburgh. James had gone with Sally's mother and father and Kevin. He wasn't keen on them going just in case it turned out not to be her. All this had happened after they had left and now they were all waiting on James' return to tell them the news.

It was quite late when he arrived back. The pub was full. It seemed as if the whole village had gathered there to hear the news. There wasn't a sound from them, waiting for James to speak. He started off by telling them that yes it was Sally. A cheer went up. He held up his hand. Sally seemed to be traumatised. She couldn't remember anything. Not even her name. She was taken into a hospital to get checked. Her family had stayed with her.

The crowd fell silent. What had happened to her? It must have been something dreadful to get her into such a state. James, looking tired and upset, held up his hand. "Once more I haven't told you the worst. When she was examined in the hospital they discovered that someone had used a branding iron on her on the lower part of her back. It spelt witch. It was still red and blistered so it must have been done fairly recently."

A gasp of horror went round the room. Colin looked at Jim without saying anything. They headed out into the lounge. "Oh God," Colin said. "What are we to do?" Jim looked as though he was ready to faint. Colin squared his shoulders. "I know what we have to do."

He went back into the bar and whispered something to James. He came back with him to the lounge. He proceeded to tell him, from the beginning, what they had found in the cellar. And they believed that the only reason for it to have been broken into was to get the branding iron. They now believed that was what had been used on Sally.

When he finished talking James was silent for a few seconds then he seemed to explode. "Of all the stupid ignorant people, you pair are unbelievable. I have a good mind to charge the pair of you. In fact I just might do that yet."

Carol came into the lounge. "What's going on in here?" James, his face going from bright red to white, told her. She looked at Colin, a look of disgust on her face.

She walked out of the lounge. Colin followed her trying to explain why he hadn't told her but she was having none of it. "Don't you realize that the person who used the iron on Sally was probably someone staying in the village? And to think that we had spent all day together. You had the opportunity to tell me. Now of course James will be afraid that I am involving you too much. He will probably send me back to the station in Glasgow."

Colin thought for a moment about telling her that he had visited the house on the mountain and that he was sure it was the house of the lovely shepherdess, part of the story that Joe had told. But then he decided that she would be even more upset to think that he had kept another secret from her.

He went to bed feeling absolutely rotten. He tossed and turned most of the night. When he came down for breakfast Carol's bag was in the hall. She had been right about one thing.

She had been taken off the case but she was going to accompany James along with some of the uniformed police to search the asylum because she had been the one who had spotted the womens' tampax. She deserved to be in on the search but after that she would be going back to Glasgow.

Colin was completely devastated. What a fool he had been. Carol would be afraid to trust him. When he said he would go to Glasgow to be near her she was having none of it.

James and Carol approached the gate of the asylum. Once again the Keeper was there trying to deny them entry. James showed him the warrant card. When they got in they made straight to the office to talk to Ronald Grant MacLean. He was standing beside his desk. It was obvious that he was expecting them.

Of course the Keeper would have warned him of their arrival. He started talking. "What is this all about? You could have phoned to make an appointment. There was no need for a search warrant."

"We are searching a lot of premises in and about the village," James told him. "We have reason to believe that drugs are being circulated from this area. Now tell me Mr. Grant. Why was it decided to build this asylum here and where do the inmates come from?"

"I told you before that some were the result of an army experiment that went wrong. I believe some kind of nerve gas.

"And how did they end up here at Dunree?" Ronald Grant moved about the room. He seemed nervous. He had changed from the last time they had interviewed him. "Tell me," James asked. "Who pays for all the inmates to be here as well as the staff?" "I don't really know. I get a cheque from the bank every month and it was my cousin Sir Nigel who built it with his own money."

"Tell me, why did Sir Nigel decide to build the asylum when it caused such ill feeling in the village? And where did you come from to run this place?" I lived in China for a number of years and when I came home Sir Nigel had enough confidence in me to run this place."

As they left James turned and looked at him. "We may have to come back for another talk." They came back to the inn, Carol just to pick up her bags. She passed Colin at the door. She didn't acknowledge him. James took her to the bus. Colin felt absolutely broken. Everything seemed to be going wrong. There was no doubt in his mind that the branding iron they had seen in the cellar was the one used on Sally. And God knows maybe used on a lot of missing women in the area.

He had to get out of the inn. He wandered about the village. His steps took him to the seat where he had met Joe. He wished that he could talk to him. As if his wish was granted he saw Joe shuffling towards him. He seemed to have grown more delicate, clutching his blanket round himself.

"I'm glad to see you Colin. I have been watching out for you. I want to finish the story. It is important as I told you Colin. What happened in the past could be the reason for some of the bad things that are happening today."

Colin knew that he was thinking about his granddaughter. A young girl gone missing a year ago. He could see the heartbreak in his eyes. A year was a long time to keep hoping that she would be returned. He was beginning to realise that he would never see her again.

"Would you like to leave telling me the story till tomorrow? You will be a bit stronger.

"Well Colin," he said. "At my age there might not be a tomorrow." He pulled the blanket tighter.

"Now where did I leave the story?" Colin reminded him. "Oh yes," Joe said. "Well things went on between Mark Grant and Lucy. They were just two young people enjoying each other's company but as the summer days went on something changed between them. They both became aware of it and it led to long silences between them. Then one day Lucy slipped crossing the burn. She twisted her ankle. Mark put his arm around her to help her up and then somehow they were kissing. Lucy pulled away. "It cannot be," she said. "You are from the castle and I am a servant of your father."

But Mark pulled her back into his arms. "I love you Lucy and I know you love me. I don't care what my father says." And because Lucy was tied to the house with the pain in her ankle Mark visited her there every day helping her with her chores.

One day when Mark was getting her some supplies in the village his father arrived. Lucy was lying down resting her ankle. She smiled at him and he saw her with her innocent beauty. He couldn't control himself. He pulled her towards him, raining kisses on her. She was terrified. She struggled, trying to get him to stop but he was a man possessed.

Mark arrived back from the village and heard her cries. He struggled with his father and because he was young and strong he rained punch after punch on him till he backed away, getting on to his horse. But as he turned he threw them a look of sheer hatred.

Mark took her into his arms and quietened her sobbing. "You can't go home and I don't want to go home. We will go to the village and then we will decide what to do. Hastily they packed a few of Lucy's things. There was very little to pack.

Looking back into the room Mark realised the hardship that Lucy had lived in in that lonely cottage. But she had done it feeling grateful for a roof over her head. What a pig my father is.

He could so easily have made the little house more comfortable for her. But all that was in his mind was to possess her. They closed and locked the door putting the key on the lintel above. Then they went to untie the horse to let it roam. She couldn't take it with her. Like everything else it belonged to Sir Nigel.

They made for the village. She sat behind Mark, burying her face in his back. How could everything have gone so wrong so quickly? When she had got up in the morning wakened by the sun she was so happy. Mark had said he loved her and she knew that she loved him. She sang to herself as she went to the burn for water.

She made herself some gruel with some of her honey then fed the horse and was all prepared to go to work. Her ankle still pained her. She would go home to rest it, not going up to the top for the sheep.

The owner of the inn looked at them with suspicion when they asked for two rooms. They knew that he recognised them and was just starting to say that there were no rooms available when Mark beat him to it.

"I was in the village this morning. I heard you complaining about trying to fill your rooms. Well you are lucky that we will take two of them." He grudgingly took them upstairs to their rooms. Lucy was exhausted. Seeing this Mark gave her a quick hug before making for his own room.

It was too early to go to bed. He decided to go to the bar for a drink. It would help him to unwind. There were only two or three village men in the bar. The owner was serving. Mark tried to make conversation but it seemed that nobody wanted to talk to him. It was obvious that the owner had had a word with them. Why did Sir Nigel's son want to stay at the inn with the shepherd girl?

He had a large brandy. He felt its warmth relaxing him. He ordered another and took it up to the room with him. He thought about what had happened to Lucy. He felt such anger and hatred for his father. All his life he had tried to police him. To get a few words of love from him never happened. He had given up. But he still tried to respect him even although, hearing snippets of conversation, he knew that he was disliked or maybe even hated.

He fell into a troubled sleep. Something woke him. Still half asleep he sat up. There were two men in his room. They came towards him and before he could realize what they were at they put a gag on his mouth and tied his hands and feet and carried him out of the room. He felt that they went down the stairs then he got the smell of musty dampness. He knew that he was in the cellar.

They dumped him on the floor and he heard the lock going on the door. He struggled. He felt he would choke on the rag they had gagged him with. He felt that it was the middle of the night. What was happening? Had his father something to do with it. Was he being punished for hitting him? He remembered the look of hatred he had given him before riding away from Lucy's.

He decided that he was just as well not struggling. He was tied up too well. He thought he heard a lot of footsteps above his head. It must be from the bar. But what were they doing in the middle of the night. Then faintly he thought he heard a scream. He listened to see if it was repeated but there was nothing. It must have been the wind. He could hear it through the trap door. He sort of dozed off and when he woke a light was coming through the cracks in the door. It was daybreak. Surely now someone would come to let him out.

Colin felt his body going tense. He had such an awful feeling that he didn't want Joe to go on with the story. He looked at Joe. The tears were running down his cheeks. "Enough is enough Joe. Come on I'll take you home." But he had a determined look on his face. "I must finish," he said. "You must understand," he continued talking.

"Mark, hoping that he would be released, did not realise that maybe it would have been better if he had died in that cellar. And not to know the horror of what was happening to his beloved Lucy.

She was wakened up just as dawn was breaking. Rough hands grabbed her. Witch, witch, a crowd outside shouted. They pulled her along the road to the blacksmith. His fire was glowing. Lucy knew what he was going to do. She cried out to the crowd. Save me, save me. I am no witch. You all know me. But someone in the crowd shouted witch, witch, burn her.

The blacksmith took the branding iron from the fire and plunged it on her back. She fainted with the pain. They lifted her up and took her to the outskirts of the village where they had built a fire ready to light. She was tied to a stake in the middle and with the chants of the crowd she was burnt. A woman in the crowd shouted out "God forgive you all. You all know you have done wrong. The Devil was let loose today."

Mark's world came to an end that day. His grief was inconsolable. He knew that his father was to blame. He made his way to the castle. If he had found his father he would have killed him but he had disappeared. Thinking that he might take his own life the village doctor had him placed in an asylum. He was there for over a year and became a missionary afterwards. He never saw his father again.

There were good people in the crowd who watched a young girl being burned to death but they were swayed with the crowd and more scared of Sir Nigel. Afterwards there was a gloom in the village. People went around afraid to look at each other. Not so Sir Nigel. He became crueler.

Looking at it today we wonder why the village people stood for his cruelty but they had no leaders and they were afraid. Sir Nigel had spies everywhere and even today the ancestors look as if they could head down the same route in spite of the modern world of today.

The present Sir Nigel has the same name passed down and his only son is called Mark. But from what we hear he is a different kettle of fish from the other Mark. Very little is known about him. The village saw very little of him and of course he has a plane that we see flying to and fro. With girls going missing from Dunree and other parts we wonder, as I said to you Colin, is history repeating itself."

Colin sat on the seat after Joe had gone. He felt horror. He was glad that Joe knew nothing about the branding iron found in the pub.

Chapter 10

Colin went around feeling upset since Carol left. He kept phoning her but she never answered his calls. There seemed to be very little happiness in the village. Jim was trying desperately to sell the pub. The only thing that never changed was the four men coming into the pub night after night. He wondered about the connection they had with the Keeper. Why were they in the Keeper's house? The night he had followed them from the pub he thought that he might just follow them another night but he thought about the reaction of James and Carol and realised that maybe it wasn't a good idea.

He felt at such a loose end. The only comfort he had was walking on the mountain. So changing into his boots he set off. He decided to walk round the mountain to the entrance to the castle. Just as before he came to the big gates. He stood looking up the long drive. A voice came from in front of him. "Welcome to fast castle Colin Grant." The gates swung open. Only then he noticed a camera on one of the trees and he knew that the last time he had stood before the gates he had been noticed.

He walked slowly up the drive praying that the dogs were tied up but everything was silent. As he passed the cottage he believed was the estate manager's everything was so clean and tidy. The whole driveway and the shrubs on either side were well cared for. As he approached the castle he couldn't help being impressed. It looked like something out of a story book.

He approached the large oak doors. He looked for some sort of knocker but they seemed to open automatically. It was all a bit overwhelming. He wondered if he had done the right thing coming in. Maybe he should have turned back at the gate. Too late now.

He entered a large hall. He stood and looked around. It was a beautiful room. One could even imagine it as a ballroom. Here and there against the walls were large couches in red silk brocade. The floor was polished oak. A red carpet in the middle ran the length of the room out into a corridor. He tried to take it all in.

The chandeliers. The white marble fireplace reached up almost to the top of the wall. A large log was burning in it, almost like a tree. The sunlight coming through the church shaped windows picked out the paintings on the walls. He looked at them. They were dated back many centuries. The men were all called Nigel. He looked at the latest painting. His face was familiar. It was of a man in his early forties wearing some sort of robes. The next painting looked as though it could be his son Mark Nigel grant. So Joe was right. They were all called Nigel and the sons Mark but when the elder died the son would use his second name Nigel. And so it went on. He still kept looking at the paintings.

A voice behind him startled him. He turned and an older version of the man in the picture was smiling at him. He was a handsome man maybe in his early sixties.

"You are looking a bit puzzled," he said. "Can I help you?" Colin felt embarrassed. "Well it's the paintings. They all have a resemblance to each other. One can tell they are descendants." And while Sir Nigel smiled at him again he stuttered.

"I can see myself in them." "You are right," Sir Nigel said. "Because you have the Grant blood in you." Colin backed away from him. "No, no, I don't believe it. I don't want to have the blood from your family. I don't know about you Sir Nigel but your ancestors were wicked."

For a moment Colin saw a change in him. There was no charm. His face took on an evil look. His lips curled and his eyes became slit. In a moment he was back to the charming man. "Come with me Colin. Let's sit and have a drink. I think we need to have a talk. He led Colin down the red carpet into a lounge. He rang a bell and a servant appeared.

"What would you like to drink Colin?" "I'll have a beer but really I must get back to the inn. My friends are waiting for me there." Sir Nigel ignored him and ordered a sherry for himself. Colin looked around and again he was struck by the beautiful room. It seemed to be all gold and green. The carpet that his feet sank into was thick and luxurious in a dark green. The curtains matched it. All the furniture gave the room a sunshine look with all the sofas in gold. Here and there were cabinets filled with crystal and silver? It seemed that throughout the castle no expense had been spared. Colin sipped his beer wishing he was miles away.

He thought back to the story that Joe had told him. Now, with a glimpse of Sir Nigel's true self, he could believe that the man sitting beside him could be just as wicked as his ancestors. And as he continued to speak to him he felt more and more uncomfortable.

It was strange but he felt that Sir Nigel had just been waiting on him to arrive at the castle.

He seemed to be quite familiar with his name and he kept asking about his family.

"Your name Colin Grant. Did your father's people come from this area?" "My father believes that going back over the years that might have been the case. He wanted me to try and trace his forebears but I haven't been successful. In fact the name Grant seems to upset the people in the area. No records were available even in the church."

Once again Colin saw the look of rage on his face. He put down his glass. "Really Sir Nigel I must go." "Well if you must but I would like you to come back. Maybe there is something of interest in the library that you couldn't find in the church. After all the Grants in this castle go back hundreds of years. "Thank you," Colin said. "I really have little interest in my ancestors. We are happy in our lives in New Zealand. It was for my father. He was always interested in anything to do with Scotland. I think he would be upset to think that the Grants had such a bad reputation.

Chapter 11

"Ah Colin every family has skeletons in their cupboards." He rang a bell and immediately a servant answered. "Will you please take this gentleman to the gate?" He shook hands. "I think we will meet again. Colin thought to himself not if I've got anything to do with it.

He puzzled all the way back. It was as if the man knew everything about him. Maybe it was one of his spies in the village who kept him informed about what went on there. And immediately he thought about the Keeper. Now there was a strange man and could quite easily be Sir Nigel's spy.

When he got back he tried again to get in touch with Carol. He would be able to share with her his unease. He would be leaving soon. It was time he went home. Things were getting too complicated here. What strange fate had brought him here? To begin with it would have been better if he had joined his friends in Paris. Then he thought he wouldn't have met Carol. She was so much in his thoughts.

But when he arrived back at the inn there was Carol at the door smiling at him. He raced the last few steps and swung her up in his arms. She was dressed in a floaty blue top that matched the colour of her trousers. Her face shone with happiness. "I have got a whole two days leave. I must make up to you for being such a bitch. Sometimes the job I do gets in the way." They went into the bar and Colin proceeded to tell her what had happened when he went into the castle.

"It all seems strange to me. Why did Sir Nigel invite you into the castle? You certainly have the Grant name but so I'm sure have dozens of tourists visiting Dunree." Colin knew that it was now time to tell Carol about his visit to the house on the mountain and the strong feelings that he had felt when he went inside.

Carol, the practical one, asked him. "What I don't understand is did you not wonder why the ramshackle house was still standing after three or four hundred years." "Well," he remarked. "The first time I saw it there was a ladder going up to the roof, left there by someone repairing it."

They were deep in conversation when all the lights went out in the inn. There was a bit of panic for a few minutes then Jim produced a lantern and pile of candles which he placed on the tables.

"A bit early for a power cut. We had one when I arrived here just over a year ago but that was in the middle of winter and it was caused by lightning hitting one of the pylons." Colin went to the door. The whole village was in darkness. It was just after midnight. "Oh well it's time we were in bed. I'm sure it will be back on by morning." But by morning there was more bad news.

There had been a landslide blocking the road into the village. No one could get through to repair the electricity supply. Jim always seeing the bright side said. "Oh well no slaving in the kitchen. A cold buffet for the rest of the day."

"So much for my two days holiday," Carol said. And it turned out to be two days before the power went on. Engineers came into the pub. They were having a discussion among themselves. Coin heard the word vandalised.

He spoke to them. "Are you saying that the loss of power to the village was caused by vandals?" One of the older men spoke. "I'm positive it was." He started to go into detail. Colin suddenly had a suspicion. All the electricity generators were in the village and the village people would never have vandalised them because they depended on electricity.

I really am beginning to get paranoid, Colin thought. That was until information came that the land slide had been caused by someone using dynamite to blow the cliff onto the road. The police warned this was getting very serious. Suspicion of drugs, kidnapping and now this.

"Carol have you noticed anything strange in the bar?" She looked round. "No Colin." Then she said. "I've got it. No strange men sitting at their usual table. Oh now Colin you don't think it could have been them?" "I don't know but they are tied up with the castle and I was there yesterday. And when I told Sir Nigel what I thought of his descendants his face looked really evil for a moment. Maybe I am to blame and he wanted to prove just how powerful and wicked he could be."

Carol had a worried look. "You should never have antagonised him. He could do you harm."

Sally and the family came to the inn to say goodbye. At last they had got permission to go home to America. Sally was still in a dream like state. "When she is better the first thing we will get done is getting that brand removed from her back." It was a tearful goodbye. Beautiful Sally, so full of joy when she first arrived.

Colin and Carol spoke about it when they had gone. "I don't think Sally will ever get over it. I wish I could lay my hands on the animal who did that to her." "Colin he will be found." Carol hugged him. "I promise you. Come on let's go for a walk."

Colin was quiet as they walked. "Something bothering you?" Carol asked. "No I was thinking that it was time for me to go home and I was thinking if it could possibly happen that sometime you could join me there. You could get work in the police force there."

Carol stopped dead. "You really have been doing a lot of thinking. I know that I will miss you terribly when you go but Colin something like that can't be decided on the spur of the moment. When we are apart and we both still feel we love each other and don't want to be apart then I will go to you in New Zealand."

"Well I will have to be content with that. When I go home the first thing will be to start practicing as a doctor. Come on let's go back and drink to that." James met them. "I just wanted to tell you Carol that we are going back to the asylum tomorrow. I know that you are officially off duty but you can come as an observer. We have left Ronald Grant MacLean long enough to stew.

Chapter 12

They arrived early at the asylum gate but there was no delay this time in letting them in. There was no sign of the Keeper but the men were still working at whatever they were doing in the garden. They were taken straight to Ronald Grant's room. In the four days since they had been there they were shocked at the change in him. He looked as though he hadn't slept for days. His immaculate suit had gone and the jeans and tee shirt he was wearing were crumpled and stained. He stared at them then they realised that he was quite drunk.

"Have you come to put the handcuffs on me? he snarled at them. "Can you not leave me in peace?" We just have a few questions to ask you Mr. Grant. When we were here last some of my men when searching down in the basement found some articles of women's clothes. Maybe you could explain women's clothes in an all male establishment. "How the hell should I know," he shouted at them. "I am just here as a puppet and my dear cousin Sir Nigel Grant has taken it on himself to fire me because I dared to disagree with some of the practices running the place."

"Tell me," James continued. "What are the rooms in the basement used for?" "That has nothing to do with me. It's not part of my job. Some members of staff attend to that part of the asylum. Now if you don't mind I am going to pack. My replacement will be arriving shortly. You can talk to him if you like." With that he staggered out of the room.

So that's that," James said. "We can't pursue the matter any further. We got the search warrant to search for drugs but there was nothing. I'm sure some excuse will be found regarding the women's under things. It could have been one of the staff bringing a woman in. We will keep an open mind about it."

Colin was sitting in the bar when they got back. He had a worried look on his face. James went to the bar to order drinks. "So what's wrong Colin," Carol asked. In reply he handed her a letter. "I was just sitting here when the Keeper came in. He handed me that letter never spoke. Just turned and went out before I could ask him anything. Carol read. "It's of the utmost importance that you call on me.

There is something I want to tell you." "What do you make of it," he asked. "I don't know." Now it was Carol's turn to be worried. "Do you think we should tell James about it?" Colin thought for a moment. "No I don't think so.

I'll wait to see what Sir Nigel has to say." "But the letter isn't signed," Carol said. "How do you know it's from Sir Nigel?" "I just know," he said. "Especially as the Keeper brought it." "Will you go to the castle? Carol asked. I will go with you if you want." "No it's better if I go alone. Anyway you have got to go back to Glasgow."

So it was left at that and when James returned with the drinks it ended their discussion.

Carol left to go back to her work in Glasgow. Colin was left alone to brood about the letter. Should he or shouldn't he go to the castle? I don't think I have hated anyone in my life but I do hate Sir Nigel Grant.

I wonder what my father would think of him? He and all the generations before him were nothing but bullies, terrorising all the innocent people in the village. My surname Grant is a name to be proud of and now people look at me with something like fear when I tell them my name. All these thoughts were going through his head. Then he remembered his father saying to him when he was a boy. Grant is a name to be proud of Colin. Never disgrace it. You know our motto is Stand-fast and remember it when things get difficult for you.

Colin felt as though his father was talking to him and his mind was made up. He would go to the castle and confront Sir Nigel. What on earth could he possibly want to tell him? He decided to walk round the hill towards the castle gates. He looked out for the marks of the strange vehicle but there was nothing to be seen. The scree on the mountain was always moving. Any marks are soon covered.

He arrived as before at the large gates. He just pushed them and they opened. Obviously he was expected. As before he made his way up the long drive.

When he arrived at the door he was surprised that it was Sir Nigel himself who welcomed him. He was indeed a handsome man. He was dressed casually in a dark sweater and dark trousers.

"I am glad you decided to come Colin. Let's go to the lounge. I have ordered some refreshments. You have had quite a climb to get here."

Colin felt like saying to him how did you know I crossed the mountain. But of course he knew the answer. Cameras would have covered every move he made.

A servant came in carrying a tray with tea and coffee and sandwiches. Colin had tea which the servant poured. He refused the offered sandwich. "Now Colin I know you are curious to know why I wanted to talk to you. Colin nodded and the first words Sir Nigel said shook him. "I know you visited the shepherd's cottage and I am sure that the few days you have spent in the village you would have heard the stories about it.

Colin said nothing. "Well," he continued. "Part of the stories are true. They are, I'm afraid, nothing to be proud of but then as hundreds of years pass they could have been exaggerated a bit."

Colin found his tongue. "I don't think that they were. Yes I did visit the girl's house and I must admit that I got the strangest feeling. As though I had been there before."

Sir Nigel actually smiled and for all the world it seemed as if it was with some sort of satisfaction. "You know I have a son Colin." Colin again nodded. "Well Mark is probably about your age but you seem to have done something with your life. Unfortunately my son has not."

"He probably had as much opportunity as you if not more. The only thing he is interested in is his plane. Mind you it has come in handy on occasion. Anyway," he continued. "He isn't interested in anything on the estate and unfortunately when I go he will inherit."

Colin wondered where all this was leading. He felt a bit sorry for the son. No wonder he had no interest. He probably knew some of the things his father was capable of.

"I want to show you something Colin. If you can come along with me." He led the way back to the great hall and started to point out the pictures of the ancestors. Colin had already noticed them on his first visit. He stopped at one.

"I would like you to look closely at this one." Colin looked. It was of a young man not long out of his teens. He was called Mark. There was something vaguely familiar about him.

"Now," Sir Nigel said. "Let me go back to your visit to the shepherd's house. You know the part where they fled to the inn in the village." "Yes I know the story," Colin said. "And after your ancestor had that innocent girl burnt to death." "That part may or not be true but her love for that man you are looking at went as a missionary to Africa. He married out there and had a son and you Colin are a direct descendent.

It took me many years to trace back. And many thousands of pounds. Look at the picture again. You can't deny it." Colin stumbled onto one of the couches. He felt shaken. He had to get out.

"This just isn't possible. How could, after hundreds of years, Sir Nigel maintain that he was a descendent. It surely must be through a great grandfather of his father. Sir Nigel had been more successful than he had been when he tried. It was quite possible that it could have cost thousands of pounds but then it was easier for Sir Nigel. He had a good start knowing that a trace could be made through the archives in the castle. He had to admit that the portrait of Mark, the shepherd's friend (maybe they were lovers) did look like him.

He had to find out more. He hated doing it but he would have to go back to talk to Sir Nigel. When he entered the castle again he found Sir Nigel still standing in the hall looking at the pictures. He spoke to Colin as if he had never run away.

"Now he was a strong man." He was pointing to a portrait. Colin realised it was Mark's father, the cursed man who had terrorised the village and burnt to death a young girl. "A strong man you say. I would call him a brute."

Sir Nigel turned on him white faced with temper. "Yes I repeat strong. He knew how to control the people in the village when they were disrespectful. Now my son could do with some of that strength.

I am sorry to say he is a bit of a weakling."

Colin didn't want to listen. He was horrified that a father could talk about a son in that way.

Chapter 13

He tried to get Sir Nigel back on the subject of Mark but he seemed hell bent on his son. "Yes as long as he has a plane to fly about in he is happy. Do you know that up in the valley there is a landing strip for his plane. It took many thousands of pounds and hundreds of men to build it. As I said before he isn't interested in the castle or the estate and there is no word of him trying to produce an heir.

"Sir Nigel you say that I am a direct heir through Mark. Please tell me how that came about." He pulled himself together. "I'm sorry Colin. I get quite upset when I talk about my son but you know already the story of Mark. He left his father and Dunree and never returned. He married in Africa and had one son. Strangely he called him Ralph. You see it was inbred in him to follow the family tradition. Well we know that young Ralph when both his parents died of a fever he had to become a missionary. He married late in life to an English lady. She died in childbirth having one child a boy."

"So what of my father," Colin asked. "Well what you are telling me you seem to have passed my father and the only reason I came to the Scottish highlands was at my father's request to trace his ancestors." "The only reason is that your father's father certainly was a Grant but he was illegitimate."

Colin felt as if he was receiving shock after shock. Hardly a day had gone past without something happening. "You can come to look at all the proof I have here."

Lying in bed at night his thought kept him awake. He went from disbelieving Nigel to believing him. What of his father so proud of the

Grant name. At least he got the name of the man who had probably seduced a young girl. Oh yes it would be a Grant all right, seducing young girls seemed to be their role in life.

No matter what he knew that he would not tell his father. There was no point in going back a few hundred years to find out that he really came from illegitimate stock. He would be happy to hear that his ancestors came from Dunree. That would make him happy.

He puzzled as well about Sir Nigel's dislike of his only son and there was never any mention of his wife. Nobody in the village had ever seen her and there wasn't one picture of her in the castle.

And in the hallway there wasn't one woman. Eventually he fell asleep but his first thought on waking was to go to visit Joe. Maybe he could throw some light on it and besides he was desperate to talk to someone about his visit to the castle.

He was sitting having breakfast when he heard the sound of a plane. He looked out. It was flying low over the mountain. It was just a light aircraft. Colin presumed that it was doing a bit of spying for his father. Once again Colin felt himself feeling sorry for him. Was he aware that his father held contempt for him? But maybe he felt the same about his father.

Joe was shocked when Colin found him on his usual seat and told him about his visit to the castle. "So it is history repeating itself." Colin asked what he meant. "Think about it," he said. "Going back to the first Mark from what we know he did not get on with his father. And the fact that a son he seemed to despise stole the shepherdess from him."

"That's another thing Joe. What happened to Mark's mother? Did you ever meet her? Nobody in the village ever saw her. It was just another mystery at the castle."

Joe's story was the same that he had thought about himself. "I would love to have a talk with Mark. Maybe he could shed some light about his mother." "You are getting into dangerous water my boy. I think you should just leave it," Joe warned him.

But the more he thought about talking to Mark the more determined he felt. If he could manage to get him away from the castle. Then he remembered about Sir Nigel telling him about an airstrip in one of the valleys. If he could get there without being seen by the cameras. He would have to plan it carefully and now was the time.

He had just flown in. It would have to be at night. He would have to get maps of all the routes. Jim would probably have them. They would be used for mountain rescue in their search for anyone missing. He told Jim of his plan but he, like Joe, advised him against it.

He didn't realise just how dark the mountain was. He didn't want to use the torch till he rounded the side out of sight of the village. After a few stumbles his eyesight got used to the darkness and he made good progress. He had a rough idea where the plane and runway would be. He knew that it would be higher than the castle. He started to pour with sweat with the effort of the climb and the fear of getting caught.

Suddenly he saw it. It had one arc light glowing, picking out the length of the runway. And there was Mark's plane. He crawled behind some rocks lying flat on his stomach. There was no one about. Why did he think that Mark would be about? He was prepared to stay there for hours but he would have to be well down the hill before dawn.

Then he heard something. He thought it was a car engine but then he realised it was the sound of a plane getting ready to land. He cowered further into the ground. What was happening? Was the owner of the plane, seeing the runway lit up, just taking a chance of landing there? Maybe it was short of fuel or had some mechanical problem.

As he watched he saw it taxiing and coming to rest beside Mark's plane. Of all the luck. He thought he wouldn't be able to talk to Mark. His climb up the hill was a waste of time and surely the plane coming down would have alerted the people in the castle.

He had just decided to give up and head home when he saw two men coming out of the plane.

They were carrying what looked like a tool box. They disappeared into Mark's plane for a moment then one of them went back to their plane. The other man stood looking around as though waiting for something. Then Colin froze with shock. Over the edge of the runway a vehicle approached. It was the strange vehicle that he had seen before going into the castle when he had followed the strange tyre marks.

It stopped beside the two men and there seemed to be a conversation between them. Then out of the plane one of the men pulled out a suitcase. It seemed to be heavy. Then the men came out of the car and took it. The light shone on them for a moment and Colin was shocked. One of the men was the Keeper and the other was one of the four men from the pub.

They all helped to take a large package from the car and placed it in the plane. The car went away and a few minutes after the plane taxied down the runway and took off. Then all was silent.

Colin just lay trying to puzzle it all out. Two planes? How many times when he heard a plane flying in the direction of the castle had he thought it was Mark's? There had been no secret of Mark's plane and in fact Sir Nigel seemed to draw attention to it.

He had even told him of the lot of money the runway had cost. He had done it for Mark he had said. And what about the suitcase from the plane? And the large package from the car. It was as if it was an exchange.

Colin thought about getting as far away from the mountain as possible. He realised that he could be in danger. He would sort out everything he had seen when he got back to the inn. He was only half way down when he heard a plane taking off. It would be Mark.

He wondered how much Mark was involved in what had gone on in the middle of the night. Obviously whatever it was had to be under cover of darkness.

He kept on, falling over rocks in his haste to get away. The first light of dawn was appearing when he arrived exhausted at the inn. There was a light on in the lounge. Jim unfolded himself from one of the couches. He was half asleep. He said at last. "I was beginning to think that (a) you had fallen and broken something or (b) Sir Nigel had got hold of you. But first things first."

He produced a bottle of brandy and two glasses. "And by the looks of you could do with it. I won't ask you any questions. Have your drink and a hot bath. It's getting bright outside. It will soon be breakfast time. I won't bother going to bed. As for you, you can sleep all day."

"I don't think I'll be able to sleep," Colin said. "Too much is going on in my mind. I will have to decide what to tell James."

"Now Colin whatever happened you know you must tell him. You know what happened when you never told him about the branding iron."

Colin slept till nearly lunchtime. He still felt stiff and sore after banging into rocks and stepping on loose stones in his mad dash down the mountain. He enquired of Jim if James was around. He told he thought he was in the police van. "You have decided to tell him then?" When Colin nodded he looked relieved.

James was in the van looking at monitors. There were two uniformed men with him. It so happened that they were looking at the mountain. Colin signalled that he wanted to talk to him. He came out and they walked a bit away.

As Colin began at the beginning of the story James looked more and more incredulous. He sat silent for a while. "Well," he said. "You have made the decision for me Colin. We were going to visit the castle but just wondering if maybe we should have a search warrant. But from what you have told me I think it's imperative that we do get one. I will go to Glasgow immediately to push for getting it by tomorrow."

Colin felt as though a weight had been lifted from his shoulders. From now on he could leave the decisions to others. Jim had lunch ready for him. It seemed that he was the only guest. They sat watching television. The news was on. Colin was just half listening when the story came on of a light aircraft crashing near Folk-stone. The pilot was killed. The crash was being investigated.

Colin jumped from the chair. Jim, alarmed, shouted. "What's going on?" As Colin made for the door. "It's Mark's plane," he shouted back. "I've got to tell James."

James was just stepping into the car when Colin came running. "Did you watch the news?" He shouted. James looked at him. "No I did not." "It was Mark. It was Mark's plane that crashed near Folk-stone." They went back into the van to see if there was anything more about it on the news.

"Why do you think it was Mark's plane?" "Don't you see? Colin shouted. "I told you about the two men doing something to his plane. You will have to inform the investigators that there could have been sabotage."

"Now Colin calm down. Don't tell me how to do my job," James said. "One thing's for sure. I won't be going to Glasgow till we find out for definite." They did not have to wait long. On the news update it mentioned the pilot was Mark Ralph Grant the son of Sir Nigel Grant, the owner of a large estate in the Scottish Highlands.

He was Sir Nigel's only son and heir. It was believed that Mark was on his way to France. Apparently he did a lot of flying between Britain and the Continent. Colin felt quite sick. Only that morning when he was coming down the mountain he had heard his plane taking off. There was a dreadful suspicion growing in his mind. His father saying in so many words that mark wasn't interested in the estate and that he Colin grant was a direct descendent through the centuries.

The horror of his thoughts made him weak. Surely no man was evil enough to kill his own son. James brought his thoughts back to the present. "Well there is no point getting a search warrant but you Colin could go to the castle to give your condolences to Sir Nigel."

Colin protested. The thought of talking to a man who he instinctively believed had killed his son. He never wanted to go back to the castle. In fact he wanted to get away as far as possible from Dunree.

From the first day he had entered the village he felt that he was getting caught in a web. Not for the first time he wondered what strange fate had guided him to Dunree. Was the desire to go there planted in his mind? It could have been through conversation with his father who was desperate to trace his ancestors.

No matter, here he was. James had continued speaking. "It would be helpful if you could maybe get Sir Nigel to talk. Something might be slipped out and you know Colin, I think the case you saw coming from the plane could be full of drugs. I think we have found the source. We have been slow realising that they could have been coming in on a plane."

At once Colin felt he had to defend Mark. "I don't think he was implicated and that was what made his father so against him. Sir Nigel hated anyone who didn't conform to his wishes."

"Remember the power cuts in the village and the landslide. I'm convinced that he wanted to prove to me how powerful he was. Remember I told him in no uncertain terms what I thought about his ancestors burning an innocent young girl."

"Do you feel that you are getting too involved?" James asked. "Yes I do," Colin said. "And I will do anything to prove that he was involved in his son's death. I will go to the castle if there is the remotest chance of finding anything."

They decided that they would take the car to the main gates. James would leave him there and go back for him. They knew that the cameras would be watching but it didn't have to mean anything. Colin just getting a lift.

The gates opened to let him through and as usual the servant took him straight to Sir Nigel. There was no sign of any mourning. He was wearing a plum coloured velvet jacket and grant tartan trousers.

Colin came straight to the point. He shook his hand. "I have come to offer you my condolences. I never met Mark but I think that I would have liked him." "Do you think so? I doubt that you had anything in common with him. He was very weak you know. Do you know what happened to his plane to make it crash?" "Well from what witnesses said it just seemed to drop like a stone.

I would guess that it must have run out of fuel." "I could believe that because as I said Mark wasn't a very responsible person."

Colin felt his hand curling up wanting to punch the cruel face in front of him.

"You will have a drink Colin? Have you thought any more about the discussion we had. You realize that with Mark gone you are a direct descendent. I think you would carry on the Grant name here in Dunree, you and your lovely girl Carol.

It's as if there was a curse on us over the generations. We seem to have few heirs apart from you. When I die there will be no one to follow." He opened his arms wide. "All this and more will revert back to the crown and we can't have that Colin now can we."

Colin turned and almost ran from the castle. He met James on his way up. "Well that didn't take you long. You have only been about half an hour." Colin replied through gritted teeth. "A half hour was too long. I hate that man. And the way he spoke to me I am convinced that he had his son killed. He didn't think he was worthy of taking over the estate. Get the search warrant James. Let's pull the evil place to bits."

There was no news about the crash. The investigators were doing a thorough job. Mark's remains were being flown back, probably landing at the airstrip behind the castle. The funeral was to be private, his remains to be placed in the vault beside all the other ancestors.

Colin's only comfort was the arrival back of Carol. She just held him in her arms. She seemed to understand what he was going through. Her feeling about Sir Nigel was the same as his.

James was arranging a large squad to help in the search of the castle as soon as Mark was laid to rest.

When Colin came down to the bar to wait for Carol there was a lot of activity going on. In the normally quiet hall a man, obviously a chauffeur was carrying in a case. A woman was stepping out of a red Mercedes. The woman, maybe in her early forties, was even at that age quite beautiful. Her hair almost white blonde curled round her shoulders. She turned and smiled at Colin out of the startling blue eyes.

"Am I causing a disturbance?" Her soft voice sounded foreign but it had almost a highland lilt to it. "You are the owner?" She said to Colin "Oh no I'm sorry. I am a guest. If you ring the bell I'm sure the owner will come." But just at that moment Jim arrived. He apologised. Mrs. Vallena sorry to keep you waiting. You have booked two rooms. One en suite and a single for your chauffeur." "Yes that is correct Mr. Dounie.

I can't keep calling you Mr. Dounie." "I am Jim and this guest and friend is Colin.

"Now I'm glad that's settled," she said. "And George here will be driving me around in the next couple of days."

When she left to go to her room the brightness went with her out of the hall. When Carol appeared Colin was still quite bemused. "Just you wait till you meet the new guest," he said. "Oh and is she pretty?" Carol said grinning at him. "Come on let's go to eat."

They had almost finished their meal when Mrs. Vallena and the chauffeur came into the dining room. She smiled at them. "Wow!" Carol said. "You looked quite bemused when I joined you and no wonder. She is something else and she must be a nice person to have her chauffeur eating with her." "Yes Carol I think she reminds me of someone."

Later, having a drink and coffee in the lounge, they were joined by Mrs. Vallena. Because she was alone they asked her to join them. "Thank you again." That beautiful smile. Colin introduced Carol. "Now you must call me Lilly." "And what brings you to Dunree? Colin asked. "Well," she replied. "That is a very long story. Let me begin with George. He is a sort of bodyguard. He is attached to the French drug squad and they believe that drugs are being circulated from some highland glens.

Carol butted in. "Now Lilly you must know that I and my commanding officer are already working on that angle." "Hear me out Carol. George will be working alongside your team. In fact I think that George is already discussing it with your boss."

"Oh really." Carol was a bit put out. "No Carol it was only decided last night. I believe you had been away. When I tell you my story everything will fit into place."

She turned to Colin. "You asked what brought me to Dunree. Well I was brought up in a small highland village not unlike Dunree about forty miles from here. My parents had a small farm. I was an only child. I think a great disappointment because I wasn't a boy.

But my father made me work on that farm. He really was a cruel man. My mother, a quiet gentle woman, was completely dominated by him. I never knew what it was like to be a girl. I was the laughing stock of the village because I had to wear boys' clothes. They were more practical my father said."

"Anyway," Lilly continued. "Enough of that. You get the picture. My mother died through, I am convinced, hard work and a sore heart at the way I was treated. When I was fifteen I ran away. Now and then when I went to the market some of the farmers, feeling sorry for me, would give me a few shillings. I had it all in the hen house. My mother knew and now and then she would add maybe a sixpence or two.

Anyway when I ran away I had the princely sum of ten pounds. I went to Edinburgh after a couple of weeks. I didn't have enough for a cup of tea." Lilly was silent for a moment, thinking back. Her beautiful eyes shadowed with the memory. She continued. She took to begging for food and sleeping in doorways. Then she started to get streetwise and when it was the busiest time in the hotels around dinner she would sneak in to wash her hair and have a shower.

She was coming out of the shower one night when she bumped into a gentleman. She looked up at him. He was so handsome in his evening suit. "So what have we here?" He asked me. I didn't answer." "Ah," he said. "A street girl. How old are you?" "I lied. Eighteen. He sort of smiled. How I grew to hate that smile." "Come with me my dear. I have a flat in the town. You can stay there for as long as you want. I am away most of the time."

"I know that I must have been naïve but remember I was a cold and hungry fifteen year old. The flat he showed me into was the last word in luxury."

"I thought I was in heaven. He had it well stocked with food and drink and he gave me a key because as he said he would only be using it occasionally. I gasped when he handed me fifty pounds." "Get rid of the rags you are wearing and buy something decent," he said. "I felt like Cinderella and I thought he was a wonderful prince. I was there alone for nearly two weeks. When he arrived back I was ready to go to bed. With the money he had given me I had bought sensible things apart from the beautiful nightdress.

It was a delicate shade of blue and it seemed to float around me. I think I must have looked good because he sort of caught his breath and a strange look came on his face. I know now it was lust. He put his arms round me and led me to the bed. I won't embarrass you my dears but in a few months I knew that I was pregnant.

He seemed to be happy about it but it was as if he took over my whole body and I felt that this child I was carrying was only his and it was nothing to do with me. He hired a nurse to make sure that I did what I was told. I wasn't allowed out of the flat. He asked for the key back. I really felt like a prisoner.

My baby boy was born in that flat. Immediately the nurse wrapped him up and took him out of the room. Then this man who I thought was a prince pushed some papers at me and told me to sign. Still confused after the birth I signed them not realising that I was signing away my baby son."

He came back into the room carrying a bag with my clothes. He made me get up and more or less threw me into the street. I think I collapsed there. I woke up in a hospital. I had started to haemorrhage. Whoever took me to the hospital saved my life.

When I recovered I realised that the only place I could get food and shelter was working in a hotel and that my dear is my story, or most of it.

Funnily enough it was in an hotel I met my husband Jacque Vallena, a wonderful Frenchman. And oh until a year ago we had the most wonderful life in France. I am still lost without him. I can't believe that he has gone. But throughout the years I kept in touch with my son. When he was older he would visit Jacque and I in France. His father never knew. I think maybe you have guessed. Mark was my dear son and Sir Nigel his father. It was on television that I learned of his plane crash. I went immediately to Folk-stone. I was allowed to see his body and to get a priest to bless him so that Chapter is closed.

But now the bitterness I feel for his father can only be laid to rest when I confront him about his evil ways. Mark refused to carry drugs in his plane. This is why his father hated him. He couldn't bear anyone going against him. Oh yes, something I must tell you. I have a dear friend in the village that helped Mark and I to communicate before he learned to fly. Notes were left in the little shepherdess cottage on the mountain. I will go to visit him. Maybe you have met. His name is Joe. He can't climb the mountain anymore but God bless you Joe."

Chapter 14

James and the chauffeur came into the lounge to join them. "We have been having a discussion. We believe that Mark's internment would have been carried out today and the search warrant has arrived from Glasgow so we can carry out the search tomorrow morning." He turned to Lilly.

"I am very sorry but the results of your son's crash found that it was sabotage. His fuel pump had been slit just slightly. He would have been losing fuel at a slow rate. He wouldn't have noticed it." Lilly nodded. "I suspected it." She excused herself. "I'm very tired. I'll go to bed. I shall see you all at breakfast."

"I hope something will be found Carol. I think we all need to put closure on this drug thing. There are so many things going on now. We have a father instrumental in killing his son. But could it ever be proved. The two men would maybe never be traced."

The next morning after breakfast James, Carol, George and four uniformed officers set out for the castle. Lilly appeared looking pale. She only had some orange juice. Colin thought again how beautiful she looked. What a fool Sir Nigel was. He could have had a beautiful kind wife and son.

She asked Colin if he would go with her to see Joe. When they arrived at his house his daughter wasn't keen to let them talk to him. "He is very weak. Please just stay a couple of minutes."

He was propped up in bed, his breathing laboured. He smiled at Colin and when he introduced Lilly his face lit up. "I have waited many years to meet you. Mark will be so happy." They couldn't tell him. His mind seemed to wander. "Yes quite a climb to the shepherd's house but she was always there to help me. Dear Lucy."

They left him. He was smiling. He died shortly afterwards.

When the police team came back to the inn there were grim faces. They found absolutely nothing. For a man who had just lost a son he was in fine form ordering food and drink for them all. When they refused Carol made a point of going to the hall to see Mark's portrait. "You are right Colin There is a strong resemblance to you but also to his mother."

Sir Nigel came into the hall. "So you have found all the ancestors" "Yes," Carol told him. "Quite impressive but where are all the women? Mark's mother for instance." Just as before with Colin, Carol saw his face change into something ugly. "If you are all finished searching my home will you please go?" He was no longer the charming man. When leaving they passed the cottage of presumably the factor. He stared at them, a strange expression on his face. Carol thought it was of relief that they were going away empty handed.

A message had come in from America from Kevin to tell them that Sally had said a few words. She had repeated them over and over 'from the ground'. Maybe they could make sense of it. But they were hopeful that it could be the start of her getting her memory back.

Carol was excused from work and they wandered through the village to what they had started calling Joe's seat. "Talk to me about New Zealand," Carol said. So Colin talked about his mother and father, about the friendly people. All the little stories about his childhood and growing up feeling safe and loved. "You know that I have made up my mind Colin. I want to go there with you." Colin hugged and kissed her. It had turned out a good day after all.

The day of Joe's funeral turned out bright and sunny. The whole village turned out for it. He was much loved. It was held in the village square. The minister had just started to speak when there was the sound of a horse racing down the street. It was Sir Nigel. Everyone went silent. He rode right to the front of the crowd.

He looked around then he spotted Joe's family. He pointed his riding whip at them. "You are traitors. You live in my house and you besmirch my name. When you bury him." He pointed his riding whip at Joe's coffin. "You will go and pack your things and leave my house and my village."

"I think not Nigel," a gentle voice said. "You will leave these people alone." Lilly stood in front of him, the sun shining on her beautiful hair. She was so beautiful almost ethereal. "If you do harm to any of these village people I will tell them my story. But of course Nigel you don't recognise me."

She turned to the crowd. "I am Mark's mother Lilly. Now Nigel shall I tell my story to them. It's your decision." Nigel sat on his horse as if frozen then turned and rode away. The minister held up his hand. "Now we will continue with the service. We will sing the Lord's my Shepherd." The voices rose up to the mountain with joy.

There were tears of happiness. This beautiful woman in just a few words had released them from Sir Nigel's oppression. "The old saying if you give respect you get respect back," said the minister. The service over them left with sound of the pipes playing the Flowers of the Forest.

The villagers could talk of nothing else but Joe's funeral and Nigel's appearance. In some ways Lilly's appearance and the way she spoke to Nigel seemed to give them some courage. The man they had all feared was after all just a man. Let him do his worst. No matter what he would do they would stand together. He could maybe evict one family from their cottage but he couldn't evict the whole village.

Mark's mother, the beautiful Lilly, left the next day. It was so sad that she had lost Mark. Colin was sure that Mark had made a decision to leave Dunree and a cold hearted father. In some ways the atmosphere in the village seemed to change.

People would meet in the street instead of scurrying away indoors. They would stand and blether, not caring about Sir Nigel's spies reporting all their movements to him.

That night another letter came to him from Sir Nigel. It is important that I talk to you it said. Could you come to the castle tomorrow? "Will you go?" Carol asked him. "No way. I don't want to set foot in that place again." "Good for you Colin.

But do you know I still think he had something to do with the drugs passing through the village. We would never have been suspicious if that lorry hadn't broken down. Maybe there had been dozens of lorries taking that route."

The next day was beautiful. The sun was really warm. Because it was a Saturday people were out moving around. A couple living on the outskirts of the village, a Mr. and Mrs. Laurie and their five year old daughter decided to enjoy the day getting out of the house and going for a walk.

They were walking along the road near the car park where Sally's car was found. Their little girl Katy was skipping ahead picking up bits and pieces that caught her eye. Just off the road she saw something shining. It was stuck in the cover of a drain. Her parents called her. "Come on Katy." But she paid no attention.

She continued to pull at the shining thing. Her father went down to see what she was pulling and Katy was right. It was shining. It was a gold locket. Its chain was stuck in the large concrete drain cover. He tried to lift it but it was too heavy. He looked around for something to wedge it open.

He found a bit of an old iron fence and managed to prise it to the side. He pulled out the chain and looked down expecting to see the drain full of water. But instead there were steps going down and because he had been one of the village searchers something hit him. It was just a drain and nobody thought about pulling the lid away.

He opened the locket and thought he recognised the man and woman's picture inside. He had to persuade Katy to give it to him promising that she would get something nice when they returned to the village.

They turned back and went straight to the police caravan. James and Carol were both there. Immediately they told them the story they set off with the uniformed officers. Mr. Laurie went with them. "Yes," James told him on the way. "The two people in the locket are Sally's mother and father."

They pulled the concrete cover right over and there were the steps. The tunnel was quite wide. They'd had the presence of mind to take a torch. They walked a long distance. Carol thought they would never come to the end but then in front of them was a door. It seemed to be made of metal.

They pulled it and it opened smoothly as though it had been well used. Another shorter tunnel took them to another steel door. As before it opened easily. They found themselves in a corridor and after crouching in the drain they found they could stand upright. They saw lights in the walls and followed them along. It took them into a cellar that James and Carol recognised. It was in the asylum.

Opposite them were two doors. They were locked. They turned back and found a stone staircase that took them along to the corridor that led to the room they had interviewed Ronald Grant MacLean in. They knocked at the door. A man was at a desk. "What on earth. What are you doing here," he shouted at them.

Chapter 15

Of course Ronald Grant MacLean had taken off like a scared rabbit and this was his replacement. James didn't beat about the bush. "You know this building well?" he asked him. "I know you are a replacement for Ronald." "Yes, I am John MacIntyre. I am a qualified nurse for mental patients.

And what did you mean by asking if I knew this building well? Of course I know it well." "Well Mr. John MacIntyre could you please let us have the keys to the rooms in the basement."

"Well," he stuttered. "I really don't have the keys to the rooms down there.

"Well," James pressed him. "Who has the keys?"

James MacIntyre was getting more and more uncomfortable. "Maybe some of the nursing staff. And anyway do you have a search warrant?"

"Yes," James said. "Indeed we do." John shrugged his shoulders as if to say I've had enough. He went into the desk drawer and pulled out a bunch of keys.

"You won't be disappearing like your predecessor Mr. MacIntyre because I think we may still have a few questions to put to you."

They went back to the basement. All the keys were labeled. There was very little to see when they entered the first room. A bed, a toilet and a wash basin. Carol punched at a wall. "Padded," she said. She pulled the mattress from the bed. Straps attached to the frame would have gone round the unfortunate person on the bed.

The second room was the same. Not a lot to see except that in that room there was a chair with straps that would go round a chest and ankles. Looking closely some flakes that looked like rust was stuck to the chair. James walked around it then carefully he removed the flakes into an envelope. "I could guess that this was where they were tied to get branded. I'll get this to the lab. Can you see the picture forming?" he asked turning to Carol.

"Yes," she said. "I think that I can. The drain up by the lay by was used to take the abducted girls to the asylum. The village bus stop wasn't far away. Maybe the abductor kept a watch on it to get one on her own. And of course the village spies would watch for opportunities. No wonder the missing girls disappeared into thin air. And another thing James.

Remember when Kevin said that Sally kept saying the words, from the ground. That was her remembering. Maybe the cameras had spotted Sally in the lay by and they had come out of the ground, grabbed her and took her along the drain to the asylum.

It would all have been done quickly. Sally, probably in a state of shock would just have stood watching as she thought coming out of the ground these men. The poor girl Carol thought. No wonder she had gone into shock and lost her memory. But thank God it would seem that it was coming back.

James made the decision. They went back to John MacIntyre and arrested him on suspicion of kidnapping. A warrant was also sent out for the arrest of Ronald Grant MacLean. The rooms in the cellar were sealed off.

"Well," he said when they sat discussing all that happened. "If it wasn't for the sharp eyes of a child we would maybe never have found the tunnel. And something else," he continued. "Just how many young girls have gone missing not only from Dunree. And remember the asylum wasn't built so where did they get taken too.

We still have a lot of work to do. This village could be the beginning of something that is much bigger. And of course we still have got nothing on the drugs. We are still trying to trace the plane that Colin saw and the two men. What were they doing at that airstrip? And Sir Nigel's car. What did his men carry out to the waiting plane?

Yes a lot of questions have to be answered. And tomorrow we will visit Sir Nigel again to get some straight answers. You can tell Colin to come with us. Maybe when Sir Ralph sees him along with us he might be more inclined to talk. I believe that he had sent Colin a note asking him to visit him. It seemed that he had something important to discuss."

When James asked him to go with them to the castle Colin was not quite sure. He just hated meeting Sir Ralph again but yes he would go if it would help.

When they arrived it was the same procedure. The gates opened and Sir Nigel, the same charming self, met them.

James started. "It's just a few more questions Sir Nigel." "Well I'm not sure if I can be of further help." He led them into the lounge. He waved his hand at a tray of drinks. "Can I offer you refreshment?" "No thanks," said James. "We are here on police business." He turned to Colin. "And you Colin. Are you here on police business?" "The wily old fox," Colin thought. He had established that Colin was here not just to talk to him about the letter he had sent but that he was here to help the police.

"Now Sir Nigel I'm sure you will have been told about what we found at the asylum."

"What have you found," he asked. James described exactly the drains and the two rooms.

"Oh that. I'm afraid I know nothing about any tunnel. You will have to ask the staff there. You know a lot of men get up to all sorts of things to bring in their girl friends because as you know it's a mental institution and the rules are very strict about who goes in and out."

So in one sentence he explained the tunnel and anything belonging to any girls that was found there. Carol, watching James, knew that he was furious at the neat way Sir Nigel had squirmed out. The staff were all going to take the blame for anything that was found at the asylum. James studied his notebook. "Now Sir Nigel could you explain the four men who visit the inn every evening."

"Oh yes of course. You know that they are all deaf and dumb as a result of a government experiment on an island that I am not allowed to mention. I volunteered to build the asylum on my land with government help. All the inmates if you can call them that are or were highly qualified men. Scientists, doctors etc. New treatments are being made to help them so therefore we try to keep them as normal as possible such as going to the pub after a day's work.

So that's it, Colin thought. Everything sorted out so neatly and he felt sure that if enquiries were made that Sir Nigel had done everything by the book. "One other matter," James said. "Could you tell me about a plane landing on your airstrip?" He mentioned the date.

"I'm afraid I know nothing about it. What my son got up to I've no idea." And here Sir Nigel put on a show. "You know that my son was killed the next day. He lowered his head. "I would suggest that with all the resources open to you could find the plane. Now gentlemen if that's all I hope you will excuse me.

He turned back to Colin. "When your friends go could you do me the favour of staying behind? There really is something quite important to discuss with you."

Colin looked at James and something in his face told him to accept. "Well only for a few minutes," he said. "We will wait for you by the gate. I would like to have a few words with your factor." Sir Nigel seemed a bit taken aback. "I'm afraid that he has left my employment. Some ill relative in Ireland I believe."

Well Colin we will wait for you for ten minutes. I'm afraid that I have to get back to the village. I have got some investigating to do there.

Sir Nigel smiled at Colin. "Your friends are kept very busy it would seem. Now Colin I'm sure you are interested in what I have to say to you." Colin just nodded. "Well," he continued. "You probably realise that since my son died you will be the heir to carry on the Grant name. And because of that I would like you to come here to the castle to live and to learn how to run the estate and all it entails."

Colin stopped himself from shouting at him. Instead he said in a quiet voice. "You and your estate can go straight to hell. I think that you are the wicked man I have ever come across. If I do have one drop of your blood in me I will do everything in my life to do good to counteract all the evil."

Sir Nigel's face changed to such anger that Colin thought for a moment that he would strike him. He took a step back. "I'm going now Sir Nigel. Maybe the ghost of Sir Nigel will come to help you but I'll tell you something. All the evil that has happened around this village will now come to an end. I hope that you and I will never meet again." With that he went out the door and down the drive with Sir Nigel following him shouting and yelling.

James was waiting for him. He looked at him anxiously. "Are you all right Colin?" "Yes," he said. "I'm just fine. I think that the first thing I will do is have a good drink in the pub. What do you think Carol?" "A good idea my brave lad."

James felt that there were so many loose ends that had to be talked through. He asked Jim if they could have the use of the lounge again. When it was organised they all met there after dinner. James started off talking about Sally.

"Now," he said. "We must try to think back to what might have taken place. For instance why was the car stopped in the lay by? Suppose she had just seen something. Maybe a good view of the hills and decided to take some photos and that was when the men came out of the drain."

"But," said Carol. "How could the men have known that a pretty woman was there?"

"Ah," James said. "You have forgotten that there seems to be dozens of cameras around. Sir Nigel likes to keep an eye on what's happening in his village."

"OK," Carol said. "Now what if there was a camera in the asylum. Maybe Ronald Grant MacLean saw Sally on a television screen and got two of the deaf and dumb men to go out and get her."

"Yes Carol that certainly makes sense. It does seem that Sally's kidnap was a spur of the moment thing. Then because she was an American girl and not an innocent country girl that could have taken off to the city, they panicked, and after filling her full of drugs, took her and left her in the street in Edinburgh. I think that maybe we have come up with the answer. We can find out from Mr. Grant MacLean when we find him. But why use the branding iron on her?"

"That was something else I was thinking about" There was a thoughtful expression on James' face. "Now Colin could you go over again exactly how you found the branding iron and I mean exactly."

So Colin explained from the time he and Jim entered the cellar. "Now Colin was the iron buried?"

"Well," Colin explained. "Not exactly buried. It was just sort of covered up."

"OK," James said. "After breakfast I want a few of us to go to the cellar. I want it searched inch by inch. Oh I know we've already searched it but I think something may have been overlooked. As to why the iron was used on Sally? Who can tell? Maybe just out of anger and frustration knowing that they had messed up by taking her captive. On the other hand it could have been used many times before. It seems as if whoever is responsible really hated women."

James wound up the meeting. Colin and Carol decided to go for a walk. It was a beautiful night. The air felt so fresh coming down from the mountains. No one was about. All the little cottages had their curtains drawn tight shutting out the world.

"It is such a beautiful village," Carol said. "Why has one man managed to cause such unhappiness?"

By morning they found out the extent of Sir Nigel's hatred. Every cottage had received a letter stating that the rents were to be increased to almost double. The residents were all out in the street. How could he do this? They were all completely shattered. They had less than two weeks. The rents were due at the end of the month. They could do nothing about it. They were all tied cottages belonging to Sir Nigel.

Colin knew that this last hate campaign was to do with him. Sir Nigel was letting the village suffer because he would not agree with him and in fact there had been no doubt about the hatred he felt for him. Like the last time he had defied him he had cut off the electricity to the village. No matter that Carol had said it was nonsense he knew in his heart that it was true. He was worried. What would Sir Nigel do next?

He spoke to some of the villagers. They seemed to be just wandering around like lost sheep. "Why don't you have a meeting to come up with some suggestions," he said to them. "I could ask Jim if you could all meet in the bar. No I don't think that would be a good idea. Sir Nigel would find out that Jim had held the meeting and would find some way to punish him."

One of the men stepped forward. Colin recognised him. It was the father of the little girl who had led them to the drain. "Why don't we have a meeting in the square?" Colin listened to him. Here was a leader. "Could you arrange it Mr. Laurie?" "Yes," he said. "I'll do that."

At last Colin thought. They were standing up together against Sir Nigel. Maybe he would think again about punishing them for some trivial thing. He wondered where all the hatred came from. It seemed to have grown worse. He was sure that if Sir Nigel lived in the past he would indeed have been as bad if not worse than his ancestor Sir Ralph. There would have been a lot of burnings of innocent women. But maybe there was hence the branding iron.

James, Carol and three of the uniformed policemen went with Colin to the cellar. But we already searched thoroughly in here and we decided that they broke the latch to get in. "Yes, yes," James said. "Just bear with me. I want you all to go on your knees if necessary."

So they started off foot by foot. "I've got something here Sir," one of the uniformed policemen shouted. They all gathered round him. Where he had scraped away centuries of dirt there was an outline of a door. James put his penknife into the crack and prised it open. It was indeed a trap door that maybe a man could get into.

"Now if I could get a volunteer to go down." The young constable who had found it stepped forward. "I'll go Sir." He lowered himself down. "There is plenty of room," he shouted back. "Keep on shouting," James told him. His voice got fainter and fainter then there was nothing. Colin prepared to go down when a voice shouted from the beer hatch. "It's me." It was the young constable. They helped him in. The tunnel came out at the end of the street. It was covered with bushes that had just been placed there to hide it.

James was nodding, a satisfied look on his face. Carol asked him "Why did you think there was another entrance?" "Well," he said. "There had to be. No one could risk using the beer hatch. He would be spotted. Then I started to think. The inn going back maybe for hundred years. Troubled times.

A lot of these old inns like old houses had escape routes. I'm sure if we were able to look through the plans at the castle we would find out a lot about the inn and the village.

Chapter 16

James was feeling more and more frustrated. He was convinced that the missing girls and the drugs were liked in some way to the castle. He had been more or less ordered to come to Glasgow. The Chief Constable would like to find out about progress regarding the drug issue. No mention was made about the missing girls and what had happened to Sally. Of course he wouldn't be putting the two things together.

"Well I will find out how far the search has gone to find Mr. Grant MacLean. The sooner we get him to talk the sooner we will get the mighty Sir Nigel Grant in for questioning. I'll be back this evening Carol so don't do anything. We daren't muddy the waters at this stage."

The village people turned out in the square. Very few could afford the increase in rent that Sir Nigel had issued them with. There was very little they could do except appeal to him. It was decided to write a letter and Mr. Laurie came to Colin to ask him if he would sign it. Colin was taken aback. "I don't think I can do that. I feel that Sir Nigel is taking his temper out on the village because of a quarrel I had with him."

"Yes we heard about that," Mr. Laurie said. "And we know that maybe it is true that you are a direct descendent. But don't you see Colin if you sign the petition letter Sir Nigel might be happy that you are taking an interest in his village. It would be worth trying."

Colin looked at the faces of the villagers. How could he refuse? Surely it wouldn't do any harm.

"Well if you think it will do any good of course I will sign it."

James was looking upset when he came back that evening. "Well I got quite a reprimand from the powers that be." "How come," Carol asked him? "Well it seems that Sir Nigel Grant is well in with those that seem to matter and he complained that he was being harassed by us. But don't worry Carol I explained it all and was just waiting for a few loose ends mainly to get hold of Ronald Grant MacLean. Then I was prepared to take Sir Nigel in for questioning. So the long and short of it is we have to keep on going with our enquiries whether we upset Sir Nigel or not."

Apart from the outrage of the raised rents Sir Nigel seemed to be quiet. There were no further appearances from him in the village. A week had passed since the villagers sent him the letter that Colin had signed.

Carol was determined to show Colin more of Scotland before he went back home to New Zealand. She was given two days leave.

"I would love to show you some on the islands especially the ones near the Argyll coast. Canna, Rhum Egg and Muck. They all have a history especially the island of Egg. The story of the island of Egg is very similar to the Glencoe massacre.

The story goes that the MacDonalds of Egg and the Macleods were enemies. One winter's day when the snow was thick on the ground the MacLeod boats were spotted approaching the island. The cry went out and women and children ran to a large secret cave."

"We do not know if the MacDonald men were involved. Anyway the MacLeod landed and searched the island. They couldn't find the MacDonalds. Then by chance they followed their footprints in the snow which led them to the cave. Now the cave had quite a narrow entrance and if an enemy tried to get in they were soon dealt with. Then whoever was in charge of the MacLeods suggested that they light a large fire at the entrance to the cave. The end of the story was the MacDonalds were burnt to death maybe not by the fire but by the smoke.

Not so many years ago people visiting the cave found the skeleton of a young child. Apparently it was taken and given a Christian burial.

No one seems to know what happened to the remains of the rest of the MacDonalds."

As Carol told her story, Colin listened, his mouth dropping often. "What a terrible story Carol. How could people do something like that?" "Well things like that happen in a war and the fighting between highland clans was a sort of war, each chief doing his best to look after his clan. Right Colin let's go and find a bed and breakfast. You must admit Colin it is a beautiful island."

"You can certainly say that," he said, taking picture after picture of one of the most beautiful sunsets in the world. "Thank you Carol for taking me here. It's something I will never forget."

The next day they were back in Dunree. No more progress had been made about the entrance into the asylum. James was still waiting for the results of the flakes of blood found on the seat in the underground room. It seemed that it just had to be a waiting game to get it all tied up.

The four men still sat every night in the pub. Then when everything seemed at an end James received an e-mail from the Glasgow station. A plane had been found. They believed it to be the one that Colin had seen at Sir Nigel's but there was no trace of the two men.

There was hope that finger prints could trace them. Sniffer dogs were going to be taken to the plane to sniff for drugs. Surely things were beginning to happen.

Carol went upstairs. "I'm tired. I think it was all the sea air." Colin went to have a last drink at the bar. As usual the Keeper arrived to take the four men out. The only difference was he looked directly at Colin and there was pure malice on his face. Colin felt himself shudder.

Carol didn't appear for breakfast. Strange Colin thought. She couldn't have overslept. She had gone upstairs early last night. He finished breakfast and went up to her room. He knocked her door. There was no reply. He went to turn away and saw that the door was open a crack.

He shouted again then went in. No sign of her but the room looked as if a hurricane had struck it.

Glasses tipped, bedside cabinets and lamps were smashed. Bedding was strewn across the room. My God Colin thought. What had gone on? Where was Carol? He ran to find James with two of the uniformed police. They went back to Carol's room.

"You didn't touch anything?" James asked him. Colin could only shake his head in misery. What could have happened to his beautiful Carol? They had been so happy the day before. "It's this bloody village," he shouted at James. "There is evil here James."

As white faced as Colin, James tried to calm him down.

"We will find her." He banged his fist on the door. "We will find her. Go downstairs Colin. Leave us to do our work.

Colin sat in the bar, his head in his hands. It's him. It's Sir Nigel paying me back for putting my name on the villagers' petition. He remembered the look of malice that the Keeper had on his face when he looked at him. James came downstairs. "There is no doubt Colin. She has been abducted, her uniform thrown on the floor in contempt of the police.

In a matter of a few hours a consignment of police arrived from Glasgow. Once again the lounge in the inn was used to delegate the search. James drew Colin aside. "Whoever took Carol didn't break into her room. The door wasn't interfered with. She must have let them in." "You say they." "Yes one person couldn't carry her out. And my thought are also heading in the direction that when she went into her room last night they were waiting for her."

"But surely someone would have noticed?"

"Well suppose they took her down into the cellar." "Oh God of course," Colin shouted. "They could have gone through the secret passage. Come on James let's go and look."

"Just wait Colin. Blundering around down there you could disturb any evidence."

After a talk with the rest of the group they went down. Near the entrance to the passage was a bit of disturbance but that could have come from their previous search. Apart from that there was nothing.

Colin insisted that he should be the one to go down the passage. James agreed but he would go with him. "Watch the sides carefully. If they were carrying Carol they wouldn't have much room." They went along very carefully. Here and there they found where little pockets of earth had been disturbed.

At the entrance the branches which had been put in previously had been disturbed. A bit of movement had taken place. "There," James turned to Colin. "No proper footprints but we are dealing with clever people. They would know how to camouflage them but I'm sure this is where they took Carol."

"The exit from the tunnel or passage was pretty near the street. A vehicle could have been parked ready to take them away." Colin was getting more and more upset. "What can we do.?" "Well to start with I think we will pay a visit to the asylum. They would have to go somewhere close."

Going through the gates once again would be the third time the Keeper had let them in. The four men were at work in the garden. Colin and he thought James had been thinking that they were the ones who had done the kidnapping. If not them, who? Once again they searched the rooms in the basement. Nothing. On the way out the four men didn't even lift their heads from their work and they got the usual glare from the Keeper.

Something was puzzling Colin. He couldn't put his finger on it. Once again the houses near the entrance to the tunnel were asked if they had seen anything. Maybe a car or van parked. If there had been no one had paid any attention. All they could do was keeping on searching round the village.

Colin sat in the lounge his head in his hands. He thought about Kevin sitting there when Sally was missing and the great news when she was found. His mind wandered on. He thought how happy he had been wandering about the mountain. Then suddenly a picture came into his mind.

The tracks of that strange vehicle he had followed which had led him to the castle. Where had they started from He went looking for James. He explained how puzzled he had been. James listened. "I think you might have something. It's too late now but first thing tomorrow morning we will search."

"If you can remember the spot you first saw the tracks we will start searching downhill from there." He patted Colin on the shoulder. "Maybe you have hit on something there lad."

In the morning they started their search of vehicle marks on the mountain. As James suggested they went downhill. It was very difficult finding anything even though there were still small patches of snow. As they went further downhill it was mostly hard scree. Colin was feeling downhearted and was just about to tell James to give up when there in front of him were the tyre tracks again. He followed them almost running to very near the bottom of the slope. Then they disappeared again. They were by now quite close to the Keeper's house st the end of the village.

"Right," James said. "I think we will pay the Keeper a visit. We will have to go to the asylum. I suppose he will be at work." As James spoke a van drew up at his cottage. The Keeper came out of it and went inside. Immediately James and two constables went to the door. James gave a loud knock. There was no answer. He knocked again and after a minute the Keeper answered. He almost growled at them. James very politely asked if they could come in.

"Certainly not. You don't have a warrant." "But yes we do actually," James said. Then Colin remembered James' visit to Glasgow. Because of the drug suspicions he could visit any suspicious building or house in the village.

With bad grace the Keeper let them in. The search was meticulous. The cottage had two bedrooms apart from the toilet and lounge. One bedroom had an unmade double bed, presumably the Keeper's. The other bedroom had only a single bed. It didn't look as if it was used. No bed linen on it, just a bare mattress.

Colin drew James aside. "Remember the night I spied through the window the pub men were in. They were putting on white coats."

"Yes I know. You told me about it Colin."

"Well where did the men go because the lights went out and nobody left the cottage. I thought they had all gone to bed but obviously they had not so where did they all go? And another thing when we were at the asylum early yesterday morning I saw something out of place and now I have just remembered.

One of the pub men was wearing clothes. The buttons on his shirt were all done wrongly and his whole appearance looked as if he had got dressed ina hurry. I think the answer is here in this cottage."

"Right," James said. "Let's start again." So once again they went over every corner. Absolutely nothing was found. They all trooped out. The Keeper slammed the door after them. Colin was still sure that they had missed something. He was passing a lean to at the side of the cottage. It was full of logs, not neatly filled as was usual but just thrown in any old way.

He shouted James back and they all started pulling the logs apart. The floor of the lean to had two long doors with pull up handles. James pulled one handle and Colin the other.

Before them was a large tunnel big enough to house the strange vehicle that had left the tyre marks on the mountain.

"Right," James spoke to the two constables. "The Keeper has not to leave these premises. Nor must he communicate with anyone. We will follow the tunnel and see where it comes out."

And sure enough it came out near a well hidden group of rocks not very far from where Colin had been sitting. And of course they knew that it had been heading for the castle.

"You know what this means Colin?" James said. Colin nodded. "I have always known that all the bad things happening in the village came from that evil man Sir Nigel Grant."

They approached the castle. They were surprised to find the large gate open and there standing in the entrance was Sir Nigel.

"Do come in gentlemen. I can see that my complaint to the Chief Constable did not carry as much weight as it used to." James asked him if he had any objection to them searching the castle once again. "Be my guest. You will find me in the lounge if you wish to talk to me."

They found the car or whatever it could be called in the garage. Not even bothering to conceal it. Then they began the search. One of their officers was missing and they were all determined to find her. Colin felt that he would be prepared to crawl on his knees for miles if only he could hold her and keep her safe.

Chapter 17

The castle was a huge place to search but they were all prepared to search day and night and that was exactly what they did. They started right at the top at the rooms by the battlements and slowly worked their way down. There was a squad of twenty looking but it was nearly sunrise before they reached ground level. Sir Nigel approached them. There was a smirk on his face.

"Well gentlemen did you find anything you were looking for?" He was completely ignored. They had to give up. There was nothing in the castle and James summed up Sir Nigel's smirking. He knew that they would find nothing because there was nothing to find. No trace of Carol. No trace of any drugs.

Sir Nigel shouted after them. "Colin when you can leave your friends you can come back to have a talk with me. The gates will be open. In fact they always are since my trusted estate manager left."

Colin had a thought. Why did the estate manager leave so suddenly and surely he wouldn't have taken the dogs with him? They certainly weren't safe among strangers. They were pretty vicious. He turned to Sir Nigel. "Do you have the keys to the cottage that the estate manager used?" He noticed a change coming over his face. "I'm afraid you cannot go in there. My manager would have to give you permission and as I told you he is away to Ireland."

James stepped forward. "I'm afraid Sir Nigel as the cottage is part of the castle grounds I have the warrant to search it."

A complete change had come over Sir Nigel's face. There was a mixture of hate and fear. Colin felt a sort of tingling. Something told him that they were on to something.

The cottage was as he remembered it. There was a cold dampness in it. No fire had been lit for some time. The dogs feeding bowls were beside the sink. They were both full of food. Colin had an uneasy feeling. Why had the dogs not eaten?

It was an easy place to search. Loose floor boards were pulled up. Nothing. A back door led into part of a wood. There was a sort of path. They followed it towards what was left of an old tower. Probably near five hundred years old. It could have been the original castle. An iron door was set into one of the walls.

When they managed to pull it open it led them into an underground room. Years before it would maybe have been a medieval dining room. Lots of what appeared to be bits of tapestries still hung on the stone walls. At the end of the room was a door. One that looked recently made. It stood out because it looked so incongruous in such surroundings.

They opened it and were immediately hit with a bright light. The room they were looking at was bathed in the two or three lights suspended from the ceiling. They just stood flabbergasted till James spoke.

"My God we have an operating theatre here." The more they looked around they saw that James was right.

Yet another door in a far wall drew them in. It was another large room furnished like a very luxurious lounge. To the side of the room was a small kitchen with all the best equipment. A large TV was on the wall. A curtain covered an alcove. Colin pulled it across. He stepped back in shock.

There were two beds and sitting on them with dazed expressions were two young girls, maybe fifteen or sixteen years old. Colin looked. There was something vaguely familiar about one of them. Then he remembered. The photo old Joe had in his house of his granddaughter Jenny who had gone missing a year earlier.

Something flickered in the girl's eyes when Colin shouted Jenny. She half walked half crawled towards him. She was shackled to the wall on a large chain. Colin put his arms around her. "Don't be afraid Jenny.

We are here to help you." Tears rolled down her cheeks but she never spoke. The same thing was happening to the other girl. When James spoke softly to her she cried.

"What in the name of heaven has been going on here?" They looked around in another side room. All the necessary things for a nursery. Cots, baby baths, just about everything and Colin noticed white coats hanging on a rail. The same as he had seen the pub men wearing.

All the girls that had gone missing over the years. Was this where they had ended up? James opened cupboard after cupboard with a set of keys hanging near the white coats. There were enough drugs of every kind in them.

They eventually found the keys to open the locks on the girls' chains. The chains were long enough to enable them to wander in the room, to make a meal or to watch TV. In fact apart from the horror of them being kidnapped they had every luxury. Colin found piles of teenage clothes in a cupboard. Why was it set up as a theatre? What kind of operations were taking place in this room?

"We must get them away." James spoke on the phone. "An ambulance will be here shortly. I think the best place to take them will be the inn. Maybe later when whatever drug they had been given had worn off they may be able to tell us something about this hellish place."

The doctor would be at the inn to meet the ambulance. When they left they continued the search. There were so many nooks and crannies. The sniffer dogs raced about. At one point they scraped at yet another door but it was only a cupboard full of tins of food and packets of cereal. The dogs went mad jumping up to the shelves. Packet after packet of cereal landed on the floor. The dog handler shouted at them. "Heel, Sit" He picked up one of the cereal packets that had burst open. What came out of it wasn't cereal but two bags of white powder.

"Well, well," James said. "At last the source of all the drugs. They would be distributed from here by lorry and plane into all the cities."

The dogs wouldn't settle. They kept going to the entrance. The handler couldn't understand. "They have never behaved like this. I'll let them go. They must have smelt something."

Colin went with the handler. Just a few yards away among the trees the dogs were frantically digging. Clouds of earth were getting thrown up. The dogs stopped digging. As they looked around a hand appeared among the earth. Colin and the handler shouted to the police team to come and dig. In a few minutes they unearthed the body of a man and on each side of him a dog.

The handler turned away and was sick. There were tears running down his cheeks. Maybe the man deserved it but to do that to poor animals.

Colin looked more clearly at the body. "I know who it is. It's the estate manager. I met him when I injured my ankle." He remembered how gentle he had been bandaging it up.

"I think he was attacked and the dogs tried to protect him. I knew that they were devoted to him. So Sir Nigel, he had gone to Ireland had he."

James took two of the officers with him and went back up to the castle. He banged at the door and pulled the big bell. It was Sir Nigel himself who answered the door. James realised that in all these visits there was no servant around. Sir Nigel stood smirking at them. "Good gracious can't you people stay away?"

"Sir Nigel I am here to arrest you for the murder of your estate manager and also for dealing in drugs and kidnapping." He read him his rights. "You will be taken to Glasgow. One of the constables will make your castle secure." One of the constables stepped forward and put the handcuffs on him and it was only then that they saw the real evil in him. He cursed and swore. A froth was coming from his mouth just like an animal.

Colin went back into the room that the young girls had been held in.

Maybe Carol had been held here. Oh God. He prayed silently. Please bring her back safely.

Later the next day with the doctor's permission, James and a sergeant to take notes, spoke to the girls. Whatever drug they had been given was wearing off. Probably because they were so young their recovery was quick but they were still nervous. When James and the sergeant entered the room they cowered pulling the blankets up to their faces. Slowly they relaxed. James spoke softly to them, letting them speak. Only prompting them now and again.

"I want to go home," Jenny kept saying. "Where have you taken us?" Obviously they were so drugged when they were taken to the inn they had no idea where they were.

James explained. "I want you both to tell me as much as you can so that the evil people that kept you prisoners can be sent to prison. And Jenny this is the inn. You are going to meet your parents shortly."

Jenny started to cry for the first time. "I will see my mother? Will she take me home?"

"Yes," James said. "In a little while you can go home." He asked the other girl's name.

"Katy MacColl. I am from Glasgow. I am nearly sixteen." It was as if she couldn't stop talking. "I was coming from school. I just stopped at the chippy. When I came out a van was at the side of the street. A man came out to ask directions and the next thing I was shoved into the van and taken for miles and miles.

I think I fell asleep an woke up in that room. Another girl was in the room. She had a baby. It cried a lot then two men took them both away. She was crying. I heard one of the men say I don't know why you are crying. You are going to be lying in the sunshine tomorrow and I knew they were taking her abroad. Jenny and I were going to be taken somewhere. There was an argument out in the kitchen.

It was something to do with money. Not getting enough and then something else happened. There wasn't a plane to take us. I think there were a lot of babies born in the next room and there were men with white coats and I saw blood on one of them when he came to give us injections. I thought they were doctors."

Throughout Katy's talking Jenny nodded her head. Now and again she would add something. Katy asked when could she go home. "Soon," James said.

Colin was desperate to find out if someone fitting Carol's description was seen. When James asked them they shook their heads.

They let the girls rest and went down to the lounge to go over the notes that the sergeant had taken. "Well we know that it wasn't one of the four men who abducted Katy because he had spoken. I suspect that it was the Keeper.

Later we will ask Jenny if she remembers where she was abducted. I suspect that we are dealing here with what amounts to a baby factory. Some of the young girls had been given what amounted to artificial insemination. Then the babies would be sold abroad. I suspect that the four men could be the fathers.

Think what price could be asked for a child who has a father who is a doctor or scientist. Something like that in eastern countries would be thought highly of and the poor mothers would be left in some city like Sally was."

Speaking later to Jenny she spoke of what had happened. She had just left the school bus and was a short distance from home when a man pulled up. She vaguely remembered being pulled along a tunnel then there was a room with a bed.

She knew she had been given an injection but she woke up in the room she was found in. Maybe Sir Nigel's greed saved the girls. They had not been tampered with. He would get more money for them that way.

Then of course the girls heard them talking about a plane. Of course it was too risky for a plane to come and take the girls. Now it is essential to find the two men Colin saw doing something to Mark's plane. In fact they are responsible for his death, if it could be proven.

Chapter 18

Still no sign of Carol. Every corner of the castle had been searched. Try as they could to get Sir Nigel to admit to abducting her he just smiled his evil smile. He knew he would be charged with all the other crimes including the murder of his own estate manager.

Ronald Grant MacLean was found in Northern Ireland. He was taken to Glasgow police headquarters to be questioned. He was just a nervous wreck. He admitted the abduction of Sally. He had spotted her stopped near the drain on his closed circuit television. He got two of the deaf and dumb men to bring her into the underground cell in the asylum.

That underground drain had been used a few times to take girls sometimes from the city from a van that the Keeper drove. "I had no part in all the others. The only one I took was the American girl. I thought my cousin Sir Nigel would be pleased with me but he was so angry. I thought he would kill me. He got her branded as a witch. One of the deaf and dumb men, I think it was the scientist one, gave her an injection and the Keeper put her into the van and dumped her in the city.

That's all I know. I've been a fool but I had no money and my cousin persuaded me to keep my mouth shut. He gave me money."

When asked if he would repeat everything in court his greed he would. "I hate my cousin. I don't think he is mentally well."

The Keeper was taken into custody. He wouldn't speak but there was enough evidence to convict him of the abduction of the girls. And also the evidence found on the body of the estate manager was enough to convict him of his murder. His real name came out. He was Thomas Grant an uncle of Sir Nigel. He had served a prison sentence for grievous bodily harm. Sir Nigel had given him his cottage when he was released from prison and so he became his willing slave. He would do anything Sir Nigel asked of him.

One thing followed another. The two men of the plane were arrested in France. They were brought back to Britain. They admitted sabotaging Mark's plane but said that they didn't think he would be killed. They weren't believed. The package that Colin saw them take into the plane was a young girl who had given birth to a baby. She was left to wander the streets of Paris not knowing where she was. Maybe she was as lucky as Sally and someone took pity on her.

All this heartache was caused by an evil malicious man who had the power to do good with all the wealth and position he had. Instead he chose to do the work of the devil.

Colin sat about in the inn. Everyone tried to comfort him but he had made up his mind that he would never see his lovely Carol again. He was sure she must be dead.

He took to wandering on the mountain. It was the only place that he could find peace. One day his footsteps took him to the shepherd's cottage. He felt that it was like a lifetime since he had first come across it. He found the key and went in. There was a movement on the bed.

He felt the hair on his neck stand up. The shepherdess's ghost was his first thought. He shook his head. The sun had gone down and it was quite gloomy in the cottage. He went to the bed and pulled back a bit of rotten sacking. A terrified face looked at him. A terrified, beloved face. It was Carol, only half conscious. She was tied to the bed by her arms and legs. One arm could just reach a pail of water with an attached cup but sometime she had knocked it over. There was no water left.

Colin untied her. She felt so light as he carried her outside. He laid her beside the burn and went back inside to get a cup for water. The cottage was full of a bright white light. He stood quietly for a moment. "I will do everything I can to make things right." He spoke aloud. Then the cottage brightness disappeared.

He hurried to Carol and gently let her sip the water from the burn. It seemed to revive her. She opened her eyes and smiled at him. "Colin," she whispered. He cradled her in his arms and made his way down the hill to the inn. He never felt her weight nor the distance he had to walk. He was so full of happiness.

The next day Carol was able to talk. She was still shaken. It had happened as they had suspected. She had just gone into her room when she was attacked. It was two of the deaf and dumb men. She had tried to fight them but they gave her an injection.

Colin told her about the tunnel that they had taken her through. She remembered coming to. She thought it was the Keepers cottage she was in. Then she was in a car in a tunnel. She remembered mud and stones falling around it. She woke up completely. She knew she was somewhere in the castle. Sir Nigel came to talk to her.

"Well Carol it's up to you. You will be held prisoner until Colin decides to accept to become heir to the estate." Carol remembered that he laughed. "I have done quite a lot of bad things Carol. Now I don't want to harm you. Colin will be given a choice. I am going to send for him. You will be kept as my prisoner until he agrees. I do need someone like a son. The one I had was no use to me. He had to go."

The next thing she remembered the Keeper coming in and a gag was put in her mouth. She was put in the car and taken to the cottage. And of course Sir Nigel had been arrested so there were no negotiations. And when the Keeper was arrested there was no water because he came every day just to give her fresh water but no food. The Keeper would have left her to die before telling where she was.

Now nearly two weeks later the trial of Sir Nigel and his accomplices, the Keeper and Sir Nigel both received life sentences and Ronald Grant MacLean two years for abetting. Something very hush hush went on at the asylum.

The four men were taken to another institution and an order was pinned on the gate saying that the asylum was to be demolished and to keep clear. With the help of the army the secret tunnels were blown up. The exit and entrance to the inn were completely blocked. Things seemed to be back to normal in Dunree.

Colin walked to the castle. He left Carol at the inn. He walked around it all day till he knew where every corner was, even outside to the rooms in the ruins. Next he went up to the landing strip where Mark's death had been planned. He looked down the slope to the castle.

The next day he visited the castle again. This time he drove the car from the Keepers cottage. It was packed with strange equipment. Once again he spent all day at the castle. He hugged Carol when he went back. "Come on let's go in to dinner." They were barely seated when there was the most tremendous explosion. They all ran outside. It seemed as if the mountain was exploding.

The earth shook in the village. Blast after blast went off.

"It's at the castle," someone shouted. There was one final blast then there was silence. No one spoke then someone suggested that maybe it was the army blowing up another tunnel.

Early in the morning before dawn the whole village went up the mountain.

They looked for the castle. There was nothing there. Just piles of stones. The hillside behind the castle looked as if it had moved covering what was left of the castle. Bits of the fences and the gate were found a mile away.

Everyone was thunderstruck. They all turned and looked at Colin. I am having a meeting in the square tomorrow. I would like everyone in the village to come. And indeed they did. Every able bodied man, woman and child came.

Colin started to speak. He explained about his ancestors and how now he legally was the owner of the village and the estate. He waved the papers that he had. Proof that from a long way down the line he was indeed the legal owner. A cheer went up from the villagers. Colin held up his hand.

Now shortly I will be going home to New Zealand but before I go I will instruct a solicitor to draw up leases for all the properties. You will all pay a nominal rent but if you wish you can buy the cottage you live in. You will all be responsible for the upkeep of the village church and the village hall.

There may be grants for that. My solicitor will sort all this out. I am hoping to have everything settled in a few weeks.

In its existence for hundreds of years the village had never known anything like it. One by one they all walked home trying to get their heads round the wonderful thing that had befallen the village.

Carol tucked her arm in Colin's. There was a smile on her face. "I wonder if we will ever know how the castle blew up. Maybe an electrical fault," she said.

Colin had so many loose ends to sort out. It was going to take a while before he would be able to return home.

He walked down the street in the early morning. The blacksmith was using the bellows in the forge. It was glowing red. He spoke to the blacksmith and when he nodded his head Colin unwrapped the parcel he was carrying. It was the branding iron. The blacksmith threw it into the glowing forge.

After a minute he took it out glowing red hot. He proceeded to hammer it till it was a straight piece of iron. He turned to Colin. "I have a horse coming in today to be shod. This will make a couple of shoes." Colin shook hands with him. He felt that a weight had been lifted from his shoulders.

When he had gone to look round the castle when Sir Nigel and the Keeper had been taken into custody he had walked down the hall where all the generations were pictured. And there sitting on table in plain view was the branding iron.

He could just picture the evil in Sir Nigel's face when he had placed it there for everyone to see. It was as if he gloated at all the evil he had done. But now with the help of the blacksmith the evil had gone after hundreds of years.

His next visit was to the church to get the grant name placed back in the church records. He felt that peace had been returned to Dunree as the prophecy had foretold.

A short time after Sir Nigel's trial both he and the Keeper took an overdose of pills. Someone had been bribed to get them. Money still talked. It was an easy way out for them.

When at last he started to pack he wondered at the strange fate that had brought him to Dunree. Had it maybe something to do with his father guiding him there? He would never know. He would tell his father little of what had gone on. The Grant name in the church records would keep him happy.

Or was it the young shepherdess who had been so cruelly put to death hundreds of years before who had guided him?

On their last day in Dunree he went up the mountain with Carol. It was a beautiful spring morning. Carol turned to him. "It's so beautiful it makes the heart ache at the thought of leaving." "We will come back Carol."

They approached the little valley where the shepherd's cottage had stood. There was nothing there. It had disappeared. In its place was a beautiful garden surrounded by a white picket fence. It was full of sting flowers and dozens of rose bushes which would be wonderful in the summer.

Tucked in an arbour a seat with a plaque saying 'Lucy's Garden'. They sat silently thinking about Lucy. "Do you think she might haunt this garden?" Carol said. "I'm sure of it." Colin smiled. "She will look after it well." And because they were young and in love they laughed as they ran back down the mountain.